TAHLARI

A DUNGEON LORDS® TALE

By
J.B. Coleman

REHASH
—MEDIA, LLC—

dungeonlords.com

Also by J.B. Coleman

Tahlari: A Dungeon Lords Tale
Dungeon Lords: The Lost Disciple
The Revenant's Tale: A Dungeon Lords Short Story
Dungeon Lords: The Saga Begins Collection

ISBN   979-8-9869966-9-1

Book Cover by GetCovers

Edited by the author.

1st edition

Follow Dungeon Lords

Discord – dungeonlords.com/community/
Bluesky – dungeonlords.com/bsky/
Facebook – dungeonlords.com/fb/

For Extended Lore Content:

dungeonlords.com/foe/

For my daughters.
The world can be dark at times, but you carry your own light.
Never stop believing in your strength.

CONTENTS

CHAPTER ONE
DARK RITUAL

B lood dripped around the pool of water, gathering in small puddles along the rocky edge.

Some of the blood came from the cuts on bare feet that shuffled along the jagged rocks as the prisoners were led in a straight line through the cave towards the pool. Most of it trickled from their palms where each prisoner was cut by their captives.

Treyvon ed' Lalo stood at the entrance to the cave. He hesitated a moment too long, taking in the horrifying scene before him, and felt the hard switch held by one of his captives snap twice across his back. He winced in pain, but couldn't yell. The mad men that had raided their village had forced all prisoners to drink something, something that rendered them mostly useless, save for the ability to walk and follow orders.

He could feel warm blood running down his back, but at this point it was of minor concern. Though his body was useless to respond, his inner mind was whirring like a windmill in a storm. In front of him, the line was long, made up of strong, fair-skinned young men around his age. All appeared to have dampened senses about them, like himself, and all were from the same tribe as him: the Tahlari.

A low baritone chant echoed eerily through the cave, brought about by the ones who had captured them. Treyvon couldn't tell who their captors were because they all wore some type of grotesque ceramic masks. In the dim light of the cave, he couldn't quite tell if the mask was supposed to be a snake or some type of dragon. Either way, it terrified him as the creature's mouth was open as if it were about to attack. Piercing eyes stared out through the eye slits. The gray, colorless masks lit by some form of purple glowing magic Treyvon didn't quite understand.

Screams cut through their baritone chant. The screams of the men right before they were forced into the pool, one by one, and held under the water. As Treyvon grew closer, now trying his best to keep up with the line, he could see that the water of the pool had the same eerie purple glow as the masks the captors wore. It sloshed back and forth as the men thrashed. Whatever concoction they gave them to dampen their senses couldn't keep their bodies from the instinct of fighting for air.

The entire world was a fog, and Treyvon begged his arms to move up from his sides, begged his legs to turn and run, but a chill ran up his spine and across his skull as he realized he had no control over his limbs except to walk forward when urged to do so.

Masked captors formed a semicircle within the pool, accepting the next victim into their ring as they linked arms and moved back and forth, swaying and chanting in some strange language Treyvon hadn't heard before. As they chanted, the purple light grew brighter, and a towering brute grabbed the next of Treyvon's tribesmen and forced them under the water.

Wild white tattoos ran up and down the giant's arms, legs, and torso, everywhere the eye could see his dark skin. Treyvon couldn't quite make out what the tattoos were, but could see they were stretched over wide, bulging muscles that didn't seem to have a problem thrusting any of the men into the water and keeping them there. The silhouette of the man's neck was as thick as a mid-aged tree. Treyvon only had memories of one other man who was ever such a size, and he was just a grotesque visitor to his village several years before.

Now that he was only a few people away from the pool, Treyvon's insides turned to ice. He could see clearly as Darius ed' Suna was led up to the pool by the brute. Darius had been his childhood friend in the village, son of the chief, and the champion of turgo ball whenever all the boys would get together to play. Now he walked forward in his forced march, down into the pool, helpless to resist the will of their captors.

The chanting grew louder each time a man was led into the pool. The light of the pool grew brighter as the brute led Darius forward. Treyvon watched helplessly as his old friend was grabbed by the back of the neck, with hands the size of a feast platter, and forced down hard into the water. Treyvon wanted to scream, but he knew his body wouldn't let him, and he simply watched, wide-eyed, as Darius flailed his arms, a pool of bubbles surfacing at the spot he went under, a sign that Darius was screaming and fighting for air.

Finally, after what seemed like many long minutes, Darius' form went limp in the water. Even though Treyvon had seen most of the other men walk away after the drowning, there was still a moment where he panicked his friend was dead in the water. The brute waited another beat and then pulled the limp man up with a large splash.

Darius was no longer struggling. He stood up straight, not even gasping for breath. Water and blood dripped from his body as the semicircle of cult members separated in the middle momentarily, and the brute gave him a nudge to walk forward between them.

Behind the circle Treyvon could now see stood another man, and though he couldn't make out his facial features, he could see he was much taller and thinner than the rest. He was flanked by two muscular men, and wore no mask. Darius slowly sloshed his way through the water to him and then stood before him. The man grabbed Darius by the face, saying something that Treyvon couldn't hear. After he inspected him, he was sent walking around the pool and back to the entrance where he gathered with the others who had already been forced into the pool.

The urge to turn and run was overpowering, and Treyvon kept trying to scream, but all he could do was manage a low gurgle and a mumble, his legs carrying him forward against his will as his captors urged him on. When he was at the edge of the pool, his eyes were practically bulging out of his skull from the panic of what was about to happen.

The brute waved him forward, and to Treyvon's horror, his legs were still listening to these madmen. He wasn't sure how the purple, swirling liquid was going to feel, but he hadn't expected it to feel as warm as it did. It felt somehow like energy pulsing around his legs. Like something that was alive. Ironically, it really was a pretty shade of purple. It reminded Treyvon of the fields of purple flowers that grew around the village he grew up in not too far outside this cave.

He gave the biggest moan of horror yet as the brute put his hand on the back of his neck. Treyvon closed his eyes and said a quick, silent prayer to his god, Solana, before he felt himself being forced forward in a quick whipping motion. The purple water consumed him, and he could feel the energy of it surrounding him.

The feeling didn't stay outside his body. He felt his hands and feet begin to tingle, along with the slash on his back where he'd been whipped with the switch. Something was entering him, slithering into these wounds where his blood had been trickling from before. The slithering feeling pierced him, crawling through him until he could feel it enter his brain.

Pain engulfed his entire body, and his mouth opened, finally allowing him to scream. The problem was, there was no air available to reload his lungs to scream again, only the slithering of the purple water as it invaded him. His lungs felt as though they caught fire at that point, and Treyvon thrashed even harder, unable to stand because of the brute's hand still placed firmly on the back of his neck.

With one last desperate effort, Treyvon pushed back as hard as he could into the brute's hand, but to no avail. His mind began to go dark from the lack of oxygen, and he knew it was the end. He wasn't sure how the other young men had survived, but he was surely going to die here under this purple pool of water.

His vision went totally black, and he knew he was dead. He couldn't feel his body anymore, couldn't even remember his own name. The darkness lingered. Then, as his brain winked out, and his consciousness was on the edge of non-existence, he saw it. A vision of a man. No, not a man. Some kind of demon dressed in a black cloak and skirted trousers. A demon with muscular red skin and piercing yellow eyes. From atop his head grew two thin, wispy horns straight out of his long black hair.

The demon let his mouth curl into a small half-smile and raised his hand. Instead of some sort of weapon or grotesque pendant, he pulled out a simple writing quill. Treyvon thought this odd, but didn't have time to think about what it meant, because a serpent floated through the air and encircled the quill. He watched in awe as the serpent devoured its own tail, completing the circle.

"Rise," said the demon in a baritone that was deeper than that of his chanting captors before. He let go of the quill and pushed it and the snake through the air towards Treyvon, who desperately tried to back away from the sigil, but remembered he couldn't move his body because he was dead. The symbol pierced his mind, nestling there against his will.

In a flash, light met his eyes again as water splashed all around him. He could feel the air on his skin, and could see the semicircle of masked figures before him as the water cleared his vision. They were no longer chanting, but standing still.

Was he alive? He tried to move his hand and found that now he could bring it up in front of his face. He could see the cut where they had sliced him with their knives, but for some reason, his blood was no longer red. His skin was barely its normal color; it appeared washed out, almost gray. Looking past his hand down at the brilliant purple water, he realized he could still see it moving and pulsing with its energy, but it was no longer purple. It was the same dull gray as everything else he could see.

"Come," said a voice in the deep dark. This caused the semicircle to break, and the men moved aside to allow Treyvon through. He couldn't stop himself from moving any other way but forward, happy to have use of his limbs again, but still not able to go where he wished.

As he sloshed through the water and past the waiting men, the figure in the shadows came into focus. He was a tall, slender man, draped in a long cloak that he let billow down into the water and surround him. Treyvon guessed the cape was made up of magnificent colors judging by the patterns on it, but to him they just looked dull gray.

As Treyvon stared up into the man's face, he could see his high, jutting nose, and piercing eyes. The man swiftly reached his hand up and grabbed Treyvon by the chin, his overly long fingernails digging hard into his skin. He could see tattoos running up the man's arm, but couldn't quite make out what they were in this light.

The man turned Treyvon's face hard to the left, and then harder to the right, inspecting him, smiling. "This batch appears to be much more under than the last," he said in his rich voice to another man standing on the rock on the backside of the pool. This other man carried a strange wooden staff and had robes even more magnificent than the tall man currently holding his face. Where the others wore masks, adorned atop this man's head was a hat in the shape of a snake. He was much older than Treyvon's current aggressor, with much darker skin.

When the old man spoke, his voice cracked with the age and wisdom of someone who had lived through many travesties in their lifetime. "Excellent, Chief. I told you that allowing the Virmorph to enter their blood would make the ritual take a much deeper root within them."

The slender man turned Treyvon's face to his own and smiled wide. "Good, we won't need to dispose of this batch like the last. These will be useful until we truly get the beasts we're looking for."

Staring into the man's piercing eyes sent a chill down Treyvon's spine. Trying to look anywhere but the man's face, his gaze saw something move in the darkness. Something he would have given anything to see just five minutes prior.

There, peeking over a rock on the other side of the cave were four sets of eyes. Treyvon could tell they thought they were being stealthy, but they were easy to spot, even in the semi-lit room. Someone had been watching the ritual taking place. Someone who had possibly come to help.

The slender man could tell Treyvon had seen something, and turned his head swiftly towards the direction of the men in the shadows. Thinking they were quick enough, the sneaking men tried to duck back down below the rock, but it was too late. The damage was done.

With a howl of rage, the slender man let go of Treyvon's face and barked an order in his ear. "Kill them. Kill them all."

Treyvon didn't want to kill the men in the shadows. They were here to help, but something inside him wasn't letting him turn the other way. The slender man handed him a knife, and Treyvon sloshed through the water in quick steps, bounding abnormally quickly towards the men who now knew their scheme was up and drew swords.

It was all a blur, but Treyvon somehow felt stronger than he ever had in his life as he attacked the men. He quickly stabbed one in the neck, and the man dropped instantly. Another swung his sword at him, but Treyvon grabbed the sword-wielding hand of his attacker and plunged his dagger into this man's heart. The man's body fell with his knife, but Treyvon grabbed his sword as he fell, and quickly slit the throat of the third.

Now only he and the last man stood, squaring off against one another. This dark-haired man looked taken aback at how quickly his comrades had fallen, but still looked determined to fight none-the-less. Treyvon knew that if there was any chance of getting out of this new hell, he would need to allow this man to get away.

The command in his soul was telling him to attack the man, but his will was fighting hard against it. The man was waiting for his next move, but Treyvon was fighting it with all his might.

"Go," Treyvon cried out in a strangled voice, his eyes bulging as he fought the urge to attack. "Tssk... ahh... leave... now... help...us."

The dark-haired man's eyes grew wide in terror as he realized his assailant was fighting against attacking him, being controlled by some greater force. The man gave a slight nod, gave one sad look down to his fallen comrades, and then took off swiftly into the darkness.

Treyvon stood, sword raised, and managed to loosen his grasp and let the sword fall to the hard ground with a clatter. He glanced back over at the slender man, still standing in the pool, and saw the absolute fire and burning hatred in his eyes.

Even if he were to get punished for this, Treyvon knew that letting the man go was their only chance at finding their way back to the light.

CHAPTER TWO
THE WEAKEST LIGHT

The pile of pebbles still lay useless on the table before her. Shame, rage, and utter disappointment were all bubbling beneath the surface as Lena Zurak stared down at the mound of lake rocks on the table before her. It was the only unformed rock left in the room, and she could feel all eyes on her.

She thought that by the time she was one hundred thirty-five she would have her life together, but as it stood she was still struggling with even the simplest tasks that her peers seemed to accomplish with ease. They all sat around her with their statues of their god, Solana, sitting perfectly pristine on the tables in front of them. Lena huffed and tried to ignore the eyes that were prying in on her lack of progress.

Building something simple from rocks using Solana's Light was an entry-level assignment. A disciple of The Light was supposed to be able to build temples to the god and help shelter those in need. As it was, she was already sitting in a room with elves five years her junior. Still young adult elves like her, sure, but it was still their first weeks at the Academy of Light. She should have mastered this years ago, and yet an accident as a child had left her with poor magical abilities.

All the students staring at her was bad enough, but her face flushed with red as she glanced over to the oak desk at the front of the room and saw their instructor looking at her. His look was kind and understanding, but it definitely wasn't a look of pride like it should have been, like any father would be proud to give their daughter seeing her succeed. She knew he was thinking back to the incident like she was, but she didn't feel like it was a good enough excuse for her poor performance. She felt that trying harder than everyone else to overcome her inferiority should be enough, but it wasn't.

Why did she have to save her older sister from the hydralisk when they were children?

It was a terrible thought, and one that made her feel guilty every time she thought it. Of course she loved her sister, Sable, and she would absolutely save her from the giant water snake again if she had the chance, but that hadn't made her life any easier every single day since the incident.

Lena ran her hand through her long brown hair in frustration just thinking about it. Her father, Umbra, always tried to give her that encouraging smile, knowing that Lena's faults resulted from his older daughter being alive, but Lena also always sensed pity there too. Maybe Sable should be the one at the academy then, instead of her?

She took a deep breath, huffed it out in frustration, and muttered the incantation again. It was a hard language, an ancient language, that she was still trying to learn. Learning a new language while trying to channel Solana's Light, and having a handicap in doing so sent Lena over the edge. She mumbled the words once more, and the rocks didn't so much as twitch. She slammed her fists down on the table in frustration.

The loud noise made the other students jump, and they all quickly turned away from looking at her, making the moment even more awkward. She swiped at the pile of rock, knocking many pieces down onto the smooth wooden floor, and made to get up. As she tried to stand, she felt a force on her shoulders that pushed her back down. She looked over at her father, still sitting at his desk, hand raised as he used magic to sit her back down in her chair to keep her from storming out in frustration.

"Thank you, class. Please gather out in the garden. Amazadan is awaiting you there for midmorning meditation before lunch," Umbra said. Lena stayed in her seat during the shuffle, knowing that her father would just sit her back down if she tried to move. She just waited, staring stone-faced directly in front of her, avoiding any eye contact with the other students as they shuffled out, and especially avoiding the gaze of her father that she could feel on her.

Not that she'd had any friends in the class, but as the room emptied and it was just her and her father, Lena had never felt more alone in her life. The silence was deafening, and she could hear her father's chair scrape across the wooden floor as he stood up to approach her. She was praying he wouldn't, but as he made his way over to where she was sitting, there it was: the sigh.

"Huhhmm," she heard as she felt his real hand land on her shoulder. It was the same thing he did every time he talked to her about her shortcomings with her magic and her progress at the academy. It was a mix of understanding, pity, and a little bit of disgust at the lot his offspring had been given in life. Honestly, she had secret wonderings if he was only disappointed because her poor performance reflected poorly on him as a father and an instructor.

"It will be okay, Lena," he said, trying to sound reassuring, but instead just making her angrier and frustrated. Who was he to say things would be okay? He didn't have these issues to live with. "There is a reason that humans don't wield The Light. It takes a long time to learn, and much longer to master. We elves have time very much on our side. Four-thousand good years is a long time to master any craft."

Lena finally turned to look up at her father. "Then let me leave and learn this in private back home, at my own pace. Being here, being stared at. Judged. None of this is helping me." She'd had this argument with him before, and knew it led nowhere.

"You know Solana's Light is strongest here in the plains, Lena. This is where good finally triumphed over evil at The Battle of the Ninth. With your disability, it's best that you learn where the flow of Light is strongest."

Lena rolled her eyes. "Disability. Right. If I hadn't saved Sable, I wouldn't be in this predicament." The words came out before she'd realized. She flinched, hunching her shoulders and pulling her head down in shame. She was kicking herself inside for accidentally saying the quiet part out loud. Umbra took his hand off her shoulder and marched quickly around the table to face her. His look was now cutting at her like a freshly sharpened sword.

"You can't mean that," he barked at her.

She just shook her head. "Of course I don't, Father. It's just frustrating being so far behind the other students. Everyone expects great things from me because of who I am, and here I am, unable to even assemble a tiny statue of Solana, much less serve him in any greater way."

Umbra dropped his stern look and smiled at her, pulling up a chair to sit across from her at the small table. "Solana already has a great plan in place for you, my daughter. I have known this since the incident with the hydralisk. You saved your sister's life. You have been given this challenge because you are meant to overcome it. One way or another, you are right where you are meant to be."

Maybe subconsciously she slipped up with her speech to admit her regret of saving her sister to shake up the usual conversation she and her father had around this subject? It had never wandered into the territory of how he saw her fate playing out. "Yeah, maybe," she said, trailing off. She had no idea what fate had in store for her, but squandering her life in mediocrity seemed to be the overarching plan.

"Yes, definitely!" Umbra said loudly and more chipper. He stood up from his chair and placed both hands on her shoulders. "Look at me, Lena." As she looked into the glowing eyes of her father, she could see herself reflected there. Wavy brown hair. White, plain student tunic. Long pointed nose and ears. Nothing special. Nothing extraordinary. "Your life is only just beginning. I know you will make Solana proud. Whether it's in the classroom where you can learn and teach others, or out in the world helping others through His will. You will make an impression in this world, for the good of all."

She just shook her head, hanging it down, defeated. "Who knows," Umbra kicked in, "maybe your magical prowess will suddenly blossom in the heat of the moment during The Janari Run tomorrow."

Lena's eyes went wide in shock, and her heart dropped. "I didn't sign up for The Janari Run, Father. There's no way..."

"Nonsense!" her father boomed with a smile. "I signed you up! There's something about real-world use of magic that can jog something inside you. Something that went dormant during the accident. It could be the jolt you are looking for!"

She knew there was no arguing with him. Once Umbra decided he was right on something, he didn't back down. The problem was that it was a head-to-head contest, and she couldn't even complete basic magical tasks, let alone compete against others. "Well, if you would just let me use my bow... I could block the tips and..."

Umbra's expression dropped, and his lips pursed. He did not look amused. "I really wish you would give up that nonsense with the bow, Lena," he said in a gruff voice, walking back over to his desk and stacking up his books. "Elves do not need bows. They need to practice magic, and The Light. Now please head out and catch the last half of meditation with Amazadan. Clear your mind for the tournament." Umbra busied himself with tidying his desk and paid her no further mind. Apparently, he had said his piece, and that was that.

She finally stood from her seat, gathered her own books, and threw them into her side-satchel. She made her way towards the door, making sure to give the small pile of pebbles by her desk a good kick on the way out. Lena had no intention of going out to the garden for meditation. She suddenly had a powerful urge to go shooting with her bow.

The bowstring felt like it was singing as her fingers held the string loosely around the nock point. She had found that nettle fibers had made the best bowstring and provided an excellent draw weight that wasn't too hard for her to pull. The fibers also made a tense enough pull to take down any prey she was hunting. The arrow itself was waiting on the rest, eager to be let loose and glide through the air to find its mark.

Each arrow took her only two hours to make, less if she had batch created arrowheads and fletching and stored them for later. This was down from six hours when she had first started, but unlike most other elves who spent all their time learning The Light, Lena spent her time doing what she knew she was actually good at: making arrows and shooting them exactly where she wanted them to go.

The mark that her arrows were trying to find now was that of the armored tallcutta. They frequented the woods around The Academy of Solana's Light, and were a delicacy if you could kill one and roast it. The problem for most was the thick armor plating that covered the bird's exterior. Lena assumed they had developed this thick, hard outer shell over the millennia as a defence against being picked off by dragons. It would be hard for dragon talons to pierce the exterior hide, but still a better chance than her arrow had. That's why Lena loved hunting them. Not only did they make many delicious dishes, but the only way to kill one was to hit it right in its tiny eyes on either side of its head, as the head was also covered in the thick armored shell.

Now she was standing with her back against a red maple tree as she had been for the past hour, awaiting the armored tallcutta to take their normal route through the forest as they foraged for edible mushrooms. The yellow caps that they loved to eat only grew in a clearing in the middle of the forest, thriving in rich soil and sunlight. Lena had grown accustomed to waiting around the perimeter for her prey to show up.

Just the stillness of the forest set her at peace. The sound of the wind blowing through the leaves put her at ease. The sound of animals rustling through the forest was much more calming than the complete silence of people staring at her as she failed every aspect of her magical training. She knew she belonged in the forest, but it was something that her 'civilized' father would never allow. Instead, her family had to show regality and grandeur. Things she very much despised.

Suddenly, she heard the ruffle of hard feathers she'd been waiting for. In one swift and silent movement, she rolled her back left around the side of the tree, closed her left eye, and pulled back her bowstring all in one swift movement. The middle of her right thumb instantly found its anchor point at the bottom of her right ear, giving her a perfect line of sight down her meticulously straightened arrow shaft.

There were three of them. Two hens and a rooster, which is how they usually traveled. The male strutted behind the other two as they foraged for the mushrooms they so desired. The females were usually tougher, sometimes too tough to eat. They did too much work when they foraged, and their meat was too muscular. The parading males, on the other hand, were the delicacy.

Lena slowly moved her arrowhead until it rested on the male's head. Her breathing was slow, timed perfectly for her release so as not to mess with the trajectory of the shot. She could feel the wind on her right cheek, meaning it was going to send her arrow left as it flew. She adjusted for that, and a little higher for distance. Just a slight lead on the fat rooster as he was walking slowly. Exhale and...

Before she could release her arrow, a branch snapped nearby. A quick sideways glance showed her that a deer was making its way out into the clearing. This startled her prey, and they all flapped their thick wings to take off and away from the perceived danger.

Staying calm, Lena lifted her bow into the air. More lead time as they were flying fast now. Finding her perfect shot, she released the bowstring. Her arrow flew straight and true, and her lead paid off as the male tallcutta flew right into the path of her arrow. The stone arrowhead sank right into the eye, and the bird dropped hard and fast to the ground. The hens flew off, not even noticing their companion had fallen.

Lena silently praised herself as she approached the rooster on the ground, examining her shot. She'd perfectly hit her mark, and he'd fallen in such a way that the arrow was sticking straight up, unbroken and still reusable. Those were the best shots, as making a new arrow took more time out of her day.

She bent down and pulled the shaft from the beast's eye, grabbing it by the neck and throwing it over her shoulders. She smiled as she made her way back to the academy, picturing the look of ghastly horror on her father's face as she trudged into the academy courtyard and cleaned the bird for all to see. At least the humorous thought took her mind off the impending competition tomorrow, if only for a moment.

CHAPTER THREE
THE JANARI RUN

"**O**h, so you signed up then?"

The sentence made Lena's stomach drop. Not just the fact that they were right, and she really didn't belong here at The Janari Run, but the fact that it was Daffodil who said it.

Three years Lena's junior, Daffodil had been a breakout star from the moment she arrived at the academy. She had put the statue of Solana together within her first week of being there, gotten esteem from all the instructors at the academy as she passed through all her tests with ease, and led her team to win The Janari Run her first year here. To top it off, her father wouldn't stop talking about her to her mother when they were home in Zelira on breaks.

"More of an obligation than a volunteer situation, Daff," Lena mumbled back.

Daffodil just smiled back at her, tucking a strand of long, blonde hair back behind her pointed ear. "Funny, the things we do to please our fathers," she said knowingly.

Lena wasn't sure how to react to that. Was she being nice? Condescending? Did her own father put a lot of pressure on her? Even if he did, Lena doubted Daffodil could possibly know how she felt. Umbra was a king of high regard. He had helped the Kroll family obliterate the dark kingdom of Vairtross, breaking their hold on the land and helping establish a new Krollian rule in Mt. Fluore. Even if Daffodil had an expectant and overbearing father, she didn't know the half of it.

"Yeah. Funny," was all Lena could manage before being cut off by the booming voice of her father entering the arena.

"Welcome to The Janari Run, one and all!" he exclaimed, throwing his arms wide for dramatic effect, the overly-large sleeves of his brown cloak swinging comically around as he did. "I'm so happy that you all agreed to take part in this year's contest."

Lena scoffed a little louder than she expected, and her father threw her a stern look. Next to her, Daffodil murmured, "Difference is, my father is usually proud of me."

Condescending. The remark from before was definitely condescending. Lena hated people who faked being nice just to poke fun at you.

Her father continued his announcement. "I see some fresh faces among us this year, so I will explain the rules for you. The janari, for those of you unfamiliar, is a long, rat-like creature that is fast. Oh, so fast. Not only can it run fast, but Solana has blessed it with a drop of His Light, allowing it to teleport short distances to escape any predator. That predator being you today, of course."

Lena drew her lips up and pursed them. She hardly felt like a predator, even to a small rat, without her bow on her back. Right now she was missing the weight of it, the warmth of her quiver that ran down her back. It felt cold without it.

Umbra continued talking. "Not only can the janari teleport away from you, but it can do the same when it feels threatened and attacks. The thing you have to be worried about is that when it goes on the attack, it has the ability to paralyze any predator with an electric jolt."

"Yikes," winced the girl next to her, a new elf in The Janari Run this year.

"Maybe don't join a game where you don't know the stakes," whispered Daffodil on Lena's other side. Lena rolled her eyes at her.

"I've set the janari loose in our traditional arena," said Umbra, gesturing at the scene behind him. Lena looked past her father at the arena he had set up in the clearing. It was a rocky wasteland. Brown rock spread almost as far as the eye could see. Rock spires rose impossibly high into the air. She knew it was the natural habitat of the janari, giving it a home-field advantage against the twenty-four students hunting for it. The place was a maze, and Lena knew the lack of visibility was sure to create confusion among the teams.

"It is your job to decide among your teams who will take what role. Attackers are used to stun the janari. If you can set it off its rhythm, you have a chance to catch it before it teleports away. Blockers stave off the inevitable attack from the creature when it's cornered. You must protect your teammates at all costs, for if any role is out of the game, you have little chance of winning. Healers should be protected the most, as they can unparalyze your teammates should they go down from a janari attack. And lastly, we have the trappers. These are the teammates that come out in the clutch and trap the janari within a force field. You must hold the janari in a field of your team's color for ten seconds. This is when your entire team must fend off attacks from the other teams, who will try to break your force field to free the janari and catch it for themselves."

In previous years, Lena had been designated as a healer and, much to the disappointment of her teams, had always failed to unparalyze anyone in time. Her team had always gone down early. She expected nothing different in this year's games.

"Everyone please hold out your hands while I cast the random decision spell for teams." Umbra held up his left hand and gave it a flick, muttering a few words under his breath. A ball of white light appeared, and quickly broke apart into twenty-four different smaller balls of three different colors: red, blue, and yellow. The balls of light wasted no time in racing off to find their marks.

To no surprise, a yellow ball quickly found Lena's palm. The decision was supposed to be random, and yet she was always placed on the yellow team. She wasn't sure if it was some subliminal message from her father, as magic of The Light usually manifested as yellow. She had always assumed it was her father's way of telling her she was right where she belonged, despite her magical ineptitude.

"Perfect. Guess I won't be winning three years in a row," the grating voice next to her said. Lena closed her eyes hard and turned her head, hoping that when she opened them, she wouldn't see what she knew was there. Sure enough, when she opened her eyes, Daffodil was holding a yellow light as well.

Lena glanced over at her father, who was beaming with an encouraging smile. "Random my ass," she muttered. Umbra was obviously trying to rig the games in her favor this year by giving her an all-star team. She assumed his play was that a win would give her more confidence with her magic.

"Now that everyone has a team, please head to your quadrant of the arena marked with your color of light. You will have thirty minutes to discuss your roles and your plan of action. Good luck, one and all!" said Umbra flamboyantly, throwing his arms wide again.

She ignored Daffodil's angry muttering as they all made their way to the rocky quadrant that was bathed in yellow light. Once she was walking on the hard rock, unable to see far beyond any of the rocky pillars, she could tell that her worst fear had come true. She was in fact surrounded by an all-star team. These students were stand-outs at the academy, and she recognized that many of them had helped Daffodil in her previous wins.

Daffodil spoke first once everyone was there, taking the role of team lead without asking anyone. "We obviously have a bit of a setback this year," she started, looking poignantly at Lena, "but I think we still have a shot at winning given our other strengths." Lena flexed her fingers and balled her hand into a fist. She wanted nothing more than to knock that smug look off Daffodil's face.

Around her, everyone was nodding, agreeing with their self-elected leader, and avoiding eye contact with Lena altogether. "Now, I will take attacker, as that's what I excel at. Lena, you will be an attacker as well. I should be able to make up for your lack of... well... everything."

There was a silence in the group, but as Lena looked around, she could see smirks on most of the faces around her. She was used to being ridiculed for her waning magical abilities, but it was rarely called out in the open like this. Her heart sank.

"Trux and Leroy, you are best at defensive spells, right? Skye and Hammond, trappers. Frilis and Hylar, everyone knows you kill it at healing. Make sure one of you stays close to me, as we can't lose our only attacker..."

Lena had had enough at this point. She couldn't even listen to Daffodil's strategy for the games. Her voice was grating on her nerves so much she felt like attacking the pompous blonde elf instead of the poor, hunted janari.

The hazy yellow color of their quadrant dropped away, and they knew the games were about to start. As the haze faded, yellow balls of light appeared above each of their heads, clearly marking them as the yellow team. Even though he was outside of the playing field, Umbra's voice sounded clearly throughout the entire arena. "The janari has been set loose! Go teams! Go!"

There was a mad rush as her team cut off their strategy talk and dashed around the nearest rock pillar. Lost already, Lena jolted after them, trying to keep up. She had a sneaking suspicion they were trying to lose her early and do the game without her. Despite their best efforts to dash out of sight and lose her, Lena was an expert tracker and a quick mover. She could tell by their hurried whispers and frantic glances her way that they were disappointed that she was keeping up with them.

"Focus on the game and not me, and maybe we'll win!" Lena yelled after them. Her team froze and looked back at her, knowing that their plan had been figured out. Instead of admitting it though, Daffodil just waved off her suspicions.

"You worry too much, Lena," said Daffodil patronizingly. "We're in a hurry because if we haven't seen the janari yet, you can be sure one of the other teams has."

Before Lena could answer, there was a thundering of footsteps nearby. Turning, they saw the blue team making their way around the rocks, blue balls of light glowing above their heads. The rules forbade them from attacking another team unless the janari was captured by that team. All their members appeared to be present, so there was nothing to do but let them pass awkwardly by them.

"Flank out," said Daffodil as the other team passed. "Mimic a woodpecker if you catch a glimpse. We'll know it's the signal and track it." Lena sighed as the others nodded and took off in different directions. Mimic spells allow you to make the sound of an animal as a distraction, or in this case as a signal. Unfortunately for her, it was just another spell she hadn't been able to figure out yet. Not that she could tell her team that, as they were already gone.

Alone, she let her tracking skills kick into gear. She looked down at the ground. Solid rock. No dust or dirt to track prints. Looking ahead, there wasn't much visibility, just towering spires of rock. No luck there. Now that her team had left her alone, though, she closed her eyes and listened intently. Even though she had lost in previous years in embarrassing fashion, there was one positive thing she distinctly remembered. It had always been she who had pointed her team to the janari by listening for its unique sound. The small sound of a quick pulse as the janari teleported.

And there it was. Small, and yet very distinctive. And it was somewhere... southwest. Lena opened her eyes with a snap and tore off running around the rock pillars towards the source of the sound. Within moments she was rewarded with the sight she had been looking for. The thin, long, rat-like creature was scurrying a particularly tall pillar. Its lizard-like legs allowed it to run extra fast, and it was using them to the best of its abilities. Lena's eyes could barely keep up.

She smiled, and then threw her hands out in frustration, not knowing what to do. She didn't know the mimic spell, and even if she did, she knew her faulty magic wouldn't be able to precisely mimic a woodpecker. Not knowing what else to do, she threw her hands in the air and sent up some bright yellow sparks.

The sizzle of the sparks made the janari turn its tiny nose towards her and sniff. Sensing danger, it curled up in a ball, and a fizzle of yellow light sent it teleporting off through the nearest rock pillar.

"Of course," said Lena, as the janari disappeared just as Daffodil and Hylar made their way to her.

"Are you kidding me?" Daffodil yelled at her, throwing up both hands and shoving Lena's shoulders, making her stagger back a step. "Sparks? Are you trying to make us lose?"

Lena caught her balance and balled her fists again, one snarky remark away from busting Daffodil's nose wide open. "I don't know the mimic spell, and you didn't care to ask if I did!" Lena snapped back.

"Of course you don't! You don't know anything! Why are you here?"

It was a thought that occurred to her daily, but hearing it out loud from another student made her squirm. She could feel pressure behind her eyes as instant tears built there, and she hoped against hope Daffodil couldn't see the extra glossiness in her eyes. "I..." was all she had time to say before there was a thunderous popping noise and they all looked into the sky as a red beam of light shot straight into the air.

The light was a sign that a team had trapped the janari and were ten seconds away from claiming victory. This gave the other teams a very obvious warning that they were about to lose, and often brought the teams together in confrontation, making the game more interesting.

Daffodil gave Lena a quick look of disgust and bolted away after the light, Hylar quickly in tow. Lena knew this was her moment to prove herself to her team, to aid them in a win. She ran after Daffodil and her self-assigned healer, and as they came into a small clearing where the red team had the janari trapped under a light shield, she could see that the blue team had already been paralyzed and knocked out by either the janari or the red team as they sought victory.

The rest of the yellow team hit the clearing just as Lena did, and they squared off with the red team. A quick jolt of yellow light from Daffodil knocked the red team's trapper backwards, breaking their spell and freeing the janari. Lena raised her hands to cast a paralyzing spell on their trapper, but a female elf that Lena recognized as the new student standing next to her during the rules announcement was quicker, blasting a beam of light at her and sending her crumpling to the ground.

On the ground in a heap, Lena felt like she was going to die of embarrassment. She was the only one on her team down, and from her view from the ground she could only watch as Daffodil quickly dispatched both of the red team's attackers, leaving them helpless to defend themselves. As a result, the red team scattered behind the nearest rock spires.

Frilis bent down and quickly gave Lena a jolt, unparalyzing her. "Thanks," Lena murmured to the elegantly dressed elf. Looking at the spot she had last seen the janari, Lena could see the creature was still there, its beady eyes darting around, seeing the imminent threat of the yellow team, and still unsure where the red team went, wondering what direction it should take next.

Gritting her teeth, Lena stepped forward, determined to redeem herself and stop the janari from making a run. Pulling up both hands, she muttered the words for a stunning spell, and allowed the yellow ball of light to form between her hands. She fumbled her hands awkwardly around the magic, willing it to stay active.

"No!" she heard Daffodil say shrilly beside her. "You'll scare it off! The trappers need to..."

But she was unable to finish her sentence as Lena released her attack. Somehow the rodent sensed the incoming beam of light and teleported to the side. Sensing that it was being threatened, the janari charged straight at Lena. As if in slow motion, Lena could see the glowing beast heading right for her, its beady black eyes locked on her as it brought its light energy towards her at blazing speed.

Any thought of attacking left Lena's mind, and instead she acted on reflex. In a flash, a dome of yellow light appeared around her, a blocking spell that Lena didn't even know she could cast, not having said any of the words to make it appear.

The janari ran into her shield, and she watched from inside as it was shocked and fell from the magical force field. The small beast writhed on the ground in anger as the team moved in to surround it, but this action only seemed to make the creature more furious. In a series of flashes, the janari bounced between every single member of the yellow team, dropping them to the ground at astonishing speed.

It tried once more to get through Lena's shield, and realizing it couldn't get to her, it hissed at her, its long tongue wriggling through the air as it growled in anger. With no one else to attack, the janari flashed off around the nearest rock spire.

Lena, still cowering from the onslaught of the janari, dropped her shield and looked around at her team. They were all unceremoniously spread out on the ground around her. Those that were looking towards her were glaring at her with fiery hatred, the pompous Daffodil among them. Since their trappers and healers were down, there was no way for them to catch the janari according to the rules. They had lost.

Within seconds, a red beam shot into the air again. There would be no draw of all teams being unsuccessful this year. The red team had regrouped and managed to trap the janari, even with their attackers still down. Lena closed her eyes. Her face felt flushed, and she knew she must be burning red.

Standing in the small clearing, her entire team paralyzed on the ground in a semicircle in front of her, she cracked open her eyes and saw Daffodil's look of absolute disgust.

At that moment, all Lena wanted to do was die.

CHAPTER FOUR

CRACKS IN THE COUNCIL

E lric Kroll, the King of Mt. Fluore, paced back and forth across the war room, all the eyes of the dozen people sitting at the long council table watching his every step and waiting for him to speak.

The simple golden crown on his head marked the freshness of their rule. Elric's father, King Vaaron, had brought their family north to Zaroft some forty years ago, and through their valiant efforts they found themselves in control of a kingdom in this new land.

Recently, Vaaron had died in a freak hunting accident, leaving his fifty-two-year-old son, Elric, to take the throne as the first heir to take over in this strange land. Even though he'd grown up most of his life in Zaroft within the mountains of Mt. Fluore, Elric felt extremely vulnerable in his new position as king. Mt. Fluore was the center of commerce in Zaroft, holding a mine full of a powerful type of crystal that the other kingdoms needed to provide light and power for their towns and industries. His new rule made him vulnerable to the kingdoms who felt they could take the mountain and the subfluore crystal mines for themselves.

His uneasy feeling wasn't helped by the fact that his youngest son, Reeve, and his cousins hadn't come back from their scouting mission. There had been reports of multiple raids and kidnappings within the villages of the Tahlari, the indigenous race of people that lived in the mountains and woodlands surrounding Mt. Fluore. The Kroll family had become responsible for the well-being of these tribes, and since the incidents seemed to recur, Elric had sent his son and a few of his nephews with him to find out if they could locate the culprits. That was two days ago, and there had been no word since.

Elric continued his pacing, his magnificent purple robes trailing along the ground behind him. As he had yet to speak, he was finally interrupted by his brother, Falton.

"So, are we sending a squad to find them or not, Brother?" Falton said disdainfully, palms flat on the table as he stood abruptly and glared at Elric. "I, for one, would like to know where my son is."

This stopped Elric's pacing abruptly. Staring out the window in front of him for a moment, he took a breath to calm himself. It didn't do much good. Turning slowly and methodically to face his brother and the other royals who had gathered at the war council, Elric's face remained calm, though his eyes blazed.

Elric spoke softly, but he added some malice in his tone, causing Falton to slowly shrink back down into his seat. "You think that I don't care about my son, Falton?" His eyes never left his brother as he slowly shook his head back and forth, slowly walking towards the table. "How dare you say I don't care about Reeve. Just because he isn't my heir, does not mean I would send him on a suicide mission. You know better."

Falton just sat in his chair, frowning. "Yeah? Well, Rangston is my oldest, and I'd very much like to know he's alright. A damn fool errand sending them out there after hearing news of the raids on the villages. And to help the Tahlari, no less!"

Elric shook his head again. True, he normally wouldn't want to risk his son to save the tribes folk that his father had freed from slavery in Darmark, their old homeland to the south. But his entire life had changed because they were here. Besides, they made excellent spies to send word to him about the neighboring kingdoms as they worked to unite the fractured land of Zaroft.

"It is not so much about helping the tribes as keeping our spy network intact, Brother. The Tahlari are avid traders with the kingdoms and bring us news of the goings-on around Zaroft. There is word of a civil war brewing. How can we expect to complete Father's vision of uniting the kingdoms if we can't even keep our own kingdom in check?"

Falton cocked his bald head, thinking. Next to him sat their younger sister, Jarina. She eyed Elric knowingly before standing to make her statement. "I must agree with our king, Falton. I am not happy that my sons are not back either, but we must gain control here at home before we begin working on brokering peace."

Home. Elric laughed out loud at the word. True, he'd come to Zaroft when he was eleven, but he also remembered the life they had back in Darmark. The noble life of lordship. Comfort and peace. That was until his father had burned bridges and headed north against their king's wishes. One bloody war later and their life of peace was now one of constant strife and worry. One of ruling a kingdom, and still striving for more.

"Thank you, Jarina," Elric said to her, nodding. He felt his simple gold crown shift slightly on his head, and he reached up to adjust it again. It had always seemed to fit his father better than it had him this past year. "News from the tribes is that the eleven kingdoms are on the verge of civil war over resources, the major struggle being iron from the mines of Incarta. King

Shlam of Incarta is refusing to sell, instead building his own military for the fight everyone knows is on the horizon. We barely have control of our own kingdom. How are we expected to broker a deal between Incarta and the rest?"

Falton pursed his lips in his sister's direction for siding against him and then spoke again. "How do you expect to gain control of our situation here, Brother? So far, the aggressors have been like wisps on the wind. If our scouting party doesn't come back soon, we have no leads or way of stopping them before another raid takes out another village. As you say, if we're seen not even to be able to manage a tribe of simple folk, how can we be expecting the other kingdoms to look to us to rule an entire country?"

"You'll be happy to know that is why we need to send a squad of ten to try to locate our sons and further investigate this new threat," said Elric, taking his seat at the head of the table. "While our army is weak in numbers, it's important that we secure the tribes. The flow of information is vital and..."

Before Elric could finish his statement, the doors from the throne room next door burst open. Elric turned around to see his eldest son, Rasgar, standing in the doorway, panting and wiping his hands nervously on his gray tunic. Rasgar didn't do well addressing crowds, but he spoke up none-the-less. "He's back, Father!" he said in a huff.

Sure enough, just past Rasgar stood Reeve. His youngest son's hair was all disheveled, and his blue tunic was badly ripped. Cuts and dried blood could be seen along his arms and torso as he made his way into the room. Elric's heart dropped when he realized that no one else was with him.

"Are you..." Elric said, unable to finish his sentence. The terrible silence hung in the air for what felt like many minutes before his son answered him.

"Alone?" asked Reeve. "Yes. The others..." there was another long pause as Reeve shook his head. "Everyone else is dead, Father." Elric could see that Reeve wasn't even looking at him. He was staring past him to his aunts and uncles behind him. Elric glanced back, jaw agape, at his brother and sister. His sister was expectedly crying, but Elric was shocked to see a tear in his brother's eye as well.

"How?" asked Elric, standing up and walking over to his son. He wanted to grab him and hug him tight, but thought it would be distasteful to do so in front of his siblings, who had just lost their own sons. "What happened?"

Elric led his son over to the table and down into an empty chair. Rasgar gave a little huff as he was not invited to sit, but did so next to his brother, anyway. All eyes were on Reeve and he slouched in his chair a bit, feeling guilty for being the only survivor of the scouting trip.

"Questioning one of the Tahlari villages led us to a cave on the east end of Mt. Fluore," Reeve started. "They had seen the captives being dragged off in that direction. A hunter also reported hearing odd chanting coming from the mountainside. We doubled back to the dwarven entry to the mountain, and they gave us directions through the tunnels from Petaro. Directions to a place they dared not go."

The room was uncomfortably silent. Not even breathing could be heard as Elric's brother and sister, aunts and uncles, and other trusted advisors listened intently. Reeve looked around awkwardly at all the eyes staring at him, and then continued.

"The tunnels from the city of dwarves led us to an underground pool. It was..." he paused, stroking his black, wispy goatee. "I don't even know how to explain it. The room was glowing purple. It almost appeared... magic..."

Elric threw a look at Jarina who popped open her eyes and tilted her head forward to show her brother she acknowledged the seriousness of this news.

The king leaned forward and placed a hand on his son's shoulder. "Was anyone there, Son? Were there people by the pool?"

Reeve swallowed hard. "Men in masks. They were... they were drowning people."

"Killing the villagers!" said Falton, scooting back in his chair a little as if he were about to stand again.

Reeve just shook his head. "That's what I thought at first, too. But these men... boys really... they came back up... they were alive! But somehow totally different. When they walked up to the pool, they were stiff and weak. They were pale and dripping blood. When they came out of the pool, they were... changed. Stronger. Able to move nimbly, and they did exactly what they were told."

"One of them," Reeve continued, choking down his words. Tears welled in his eyes. "One of them saw us hiding behind a rock. We were transfixed by the ritual, and planning to intervene, but we were spotted. The drowned man came at us with impossible speed. He stabbed Rangston in the neck and took his sword," Reeve sobbed. "He used it to stab Baron in the chest and then slit Bucklow's throat."

Reeve was now staring down at the table, unable to look any of his relatives in the eyes. "It's okay, Reeve," his father told him.

"No," Reeve shook his head. "It's not. I should have been faster. I should have acted. I should have sacrificed myself so they could escape. It all happened so fast all I could do was watch. I'm only here because the man let me go..."

"Let you go?" snapped Falton, standing up in a rage again. "Why did you get a free pass?" Elric could tell his brother looked remorseful for what he had said the moment the words passed his lips. He simply nodded at his brother and motioned for him to sit back down. Falton did so, looking sheepish for his outburst, but obviously grieving the loss of his son.

The young man sniffed his nose, tears falling freely now. "I don't know, Uncle. The Tahlari man looked like he was in pain, like he was fighting against something inside himself. He was human, but a dark shadow of what he used to be, grunting and yelping in pain. He told me to go. To find help for them. I didn't stay to ask why. I ran. The tunnels were winding, and I got lost. Bucklow had navigated to the pool for us, so I was hopeless to find my way. The Tahlari and their captors pursued me. I had to lie low for longer than I could keep track of. I was finally able to make it back to the dwarves and out to freedom."

Next to Reeve, Rasgar scoffed. "I should have been sent with you..."

"And you would likely be dead now too, Son," Elric said, glaring at his older son as if to tell him this was not the time for jealousy. "From the sounds of it, Reeve is lucky he's alive."

Elric turned back to the rest of the council at the war table. He growled in frustration as he adjusted his crown again to keep it from slipping off his head. "It seems that magic has returned to Zaroft. Maybe it never left in the first place."

A wrinkled man on the other end of the table slapped his fist down, his bald head shining in the light filling the room from the window. It was Elric's Uncle Bertram, a man that he'd come to take counsel seriously from after his father's untimely passing. "We are not equipped to handle such a foe as this, my king," Bertram said shakily. "Not without more help from the elves."

The king sat back in his chair, placing a thumb on his chin and a finger to his lips, thinking about this statement. It was true that King Vaaron had pleaded with King Umbra of Zelira to come help them stamp out the dark magic users of Vairtross, laying waste to the kingdom. The victory had gained the Kroll family favor with the kingdoms of Zaroft, but if anything, they still owed Umbra a favor, not the other way around. He didn't know what kind of deal he would have to make to get the grand elf king to come to their aid once more. Especially for such a stealthy opponent. They had no idea where these aggressors were, or even who they were for that matter.

"I understand where you're coming from, Uncle," said Elric to Bertram. "We don't have the proper resources to take down this enemy. I also know that Umbra has done us a great favor already in the past. There is no reason for him to help us again."

Rasgar leaned forward, excited. "We do not need the elves, Father. Give me fifty men. We will flood through the tunnels and take care of these beasts once and for all. I'll do it with a dozen if you have no more to spare."

Elric admired his son's courage. He was thirty-one years old and had much to prove. Unfortunately, he was also Elric's heir, and he needed to protect him. Especially against such an ambiguous enemy. The king sighed as he eyed his other son. Reeve had been so eager to lead the scouting party, but now he looked like he just wanted to go to his bedchambers and cry. Five years younger than Rasgar, Reeve still wanted to prove his worth, even if he wouldn't be the king someday.

"No," Elric said, to his son's chagrin. "We must call upon Umbra..."

"King Umbra is going to want something in return," Falton cut him off. "Apparently, Father only gave him his thanks and allegiance last time. We can't expect he'll go for that again and put himself and his people at risk..."

The room exploded in murmurs and quickly built to full-on verbal sparring.

"The elves cannot bail us out every time!"

"They have to see that this dark magic will spread to the rest of the country..."

"We need to find our own sorcerer to keep on staff for such things!"

"It's imperative that we don't lose any more men!"

"Silence!" yelled Elric, holding up his hand after a few minutes of listening in on the din. "I hear everyone's concerns, but I still conclude that we at least have to try. I will send a crow with our plea. With any luck, we will have an answer back within three days."

Elric looked at his poor son, Reeve, and smiled. "We cannot lose any more men to this cause, but it must be brought under control. The least we can do is try to bring Umbra back in to save us once more. He will understand. If this grows any further out of control, the fate of the country may be at stake."

CHAPTER FIVE
THE ONLY ONE

U mbra stood on the balcony outside his office overlooking the courtyard at the academy. It was a reflective place where he liked to think when his mind was troubled. Something about the perfectly manicured grass running between the stone paths brought a certain order to his thoughts. The giant water fountain of his god, Solana, fixed in the middle with one of his hands in the air shooting out the water for the fountain, brought calm to the order as well. The courtyard was modeled after the one at home in Zelira, reminding him of easier times, and of his wife.

It was definitely the calm that he needed at this particular moment in time. He was sure that The Janari Run would have been a sure thing for Lena. He'd stacked the teams in her favor, hoping that the others would carry her to a win. Even after breaking his own code of ethics to pull a stunt like that, Lena still managed to lose. And it wasn't just the loss. It was how she had lost in such spectacular fashion.

The old elf king sighed deeply, feeling the air enter and exit his body, trying to meditate on what should be done with his stunted daughter. She really needed a win, but not only that, she was a reflection of him and his teachings at the academy. It was hard enough running an academy for the only Light users in Zaroft, but when his own daughter was so inept at what he was teaching, it didn't give the magic a very good name throughout the kingdoms. If his own daughter had so many issues, then what good of a teacher was he, really?

The odd student wandered through the courtyard here and there as he looked down from above. New students and old students alike, on their way to classes, their dorm, the library. All of them busy in their tasks, and any one of them better at magic than Lena was. Umbra suddenly found himself missing his oldest son, Eldryn, who had been his star student throughout his academy years, and was now making him proud by using Solana's light to stop a war from breaking out between the kingdoms.

His thoughts were interrupted by a knock on his office door. He closed his eyes and took one last deep breath before heading in through the double doors on his balcony and entering his office. The room was in immaculate order. Papers were all filed in neat stacks. Scrolls were rolled up and categorized according to subject and what kingdom or country they originated from, all in their holders along the wall. It took a lot of in-depth study and meditation not only to rule his kingdom back home with his wife but also to be the leading user of The Light in all of Zaroft. Excellence and order where required.

As he made it across the office, he threw the door open and smiled. It was his oldest friend and second-in-charge, Amazadan. Unlike his own hair, which was completely silver, Amazadan had still kept his youthful appearance with his jet black hair and long beard, despite being the same age as Umbra. They had grown up at the academy together and had been friends ever since. Now in their middle-age, over two-thousand years for an elf, they ran the Academy of Solana's Light together. Amazadan was an excellent second-in-charge. Being dutiful as ever, he gave Umbra a slight bow when he opened the door to greet him.

"Hello, My Lord. Sorry to disturb you. We've had an urgent crow come in. It was rerouted by Her Majesty Zelira. Someone was seeking you back home," said Amazadan as he held out the letters for Umbra to take.

Umbra smiled at his old friend and took the parchment from him. "No worries, my dear friend. Please, come. Have a seat." Umbra waved his free hand at the plush chair that sat opposite his desk and waited for his friend to move towards the chair before moving around to his own chair behind the oak slab. Ever the gentleman, Amazadan waited for Umbra to sit before he seated himself with a thump into the plush velvet chair.

At his desk, Umbra pulled the top parchment from the tied bundle and read it. He recognized his wife's tight, neat scrawl across the parchment. It simply read, 'The world calls you to save it once again, Love.' The elf king smiled at this and greedily unfolded the other parchment. Not that he enjoyed the world being in peril, but it was nice that his knowledge and teachings were still wanted outside of the academy.

Umbra's eyes darted across the parchment. His mouth fell open slightly as he read. There were remnants of dark magic still in the Mt. Fluore area. Had he not done a complete enough job of the destruction of Vairtross? Had others learned their dark ways and created a mimic cult in their place? He also wondered if the Kroll family were the saviors that this country truly needed if they couldn't seem to handle anything without him.

"Have you read this?" he asked his friend. When Amazadan shook his head, he pushed the note across the desk. The note slid off the other side and started falling to the floor before Amazadan reached out with his hand. A thread-thin line of light left his hand and attached to the letter, bringing it quickly back to his waiting palm. Umbra smiled at his friend's snappy use of magic and waited patiently for him to finish reading.

Amazadan let out a heavy sigh. "You are sure this Kroll family are meant to be the bringers of peace to this land? They seem very inept at... well... basically anything."

Umbra nodded. "Yes, my friend. I have seen their downfall a few millennia from now, but they bring peace to Zaroft for millennia. Though, I am unsure how we are to get to the point of Zaroft being named after the Kroll if they can't handle dark magic threats that arise, as they are sure to from time-to-time."

"Downfall?" asked Amazadan. "You speak of the vision you had five years ago at Lena's coming-of-age celebration, or you've had a new vision?"

"Still hung up on the old vision, I'm afraid. That is all Solana has given me to work with. Frustratingly enough, the last five years have been silent when it comes to our god. It's just been worry, helplessness, and... more helplessness." He paused as he spoke, and Amazadan nodded knowingly, having discussed Umbra's frustration with his daughter's magical development numerous times.

Amazadan crossed his arms and leaned back in his chair, staring squarely at his friend and king. "So you are going to help them, then? That is how they will make it to this disastrous end in the future?"

The elf king shook his head. "I must stay with the students, and I must also begin work to prevent the scourge I see in the future from wiping out most of the land. I cannot wait for the answer to come in another vision."

Leaning forward, Amazadan sighed. "If you truly believe that the Kroll family is to become the ultimate power in the land, surely you must want to remain in their good graces. Denying them in such a time of need is hardly the way to tell them you are still a great ally and asset to their new rule." Amazadan paused and thought for a moment. "Will we call Eldryn back from Incarta and send him?"

Umbra knew the risks were too great to pull Eldryn from his mission to appease the kingdoms. "No," Umbra said. "If Eldryn leaves Incarta then peace talks with Caelum and Lystra will end. The kingdoms are restless, and civil war is all but upon us."

"So Sable, or Garrick then..."

"No, too far away to be useful. Garrick is learning to tame dragons in Dracaryn, and Sable is learning natural healing in Nevarith. Why they chose such normal vocations is beyond me."

Amazadan shook his head. "You can't possibly be thinking..." he trailed off, regretting the answer he was about to hear.

The elf king put his hands together and placed a finger on his lips, looking down at his desk in thought. "It may be just the thing she needs. Real world experience. Go get her."

His friend shook his head and rolled his eyes, knowing that this would not end well, but also knowing better than to disobey a direct order from his king. As Amazadan left the office to get Lena from her room, Umbra's mind was churning. This was a good idea, right? Lena could go there and see if the threat was worth tending to. She would get real-world experience with magic and help keep the ties between them and the Kroll family strong. He would have time to work on his studies and find a solution to the scourge that was to wipe out most of the people of the land. It would work excellently.

The dormitories for students weren't that far off the main building, and the door was reopening within ten minutes. Lena stormed in with Amazadan entering and closing the door carefully behind her. Her eyes were squinted at her father, a quick puff of air blowing a piece of hair out of her eyes.

"I see my friend here has filled you in then."

"Yes!" she exclaimed. "And apparently you weren't at The Janari Run, Father. I can't even combat a damn weasel, and now you're expecting me to go off and fight a cult of dark magic users?"

Umbra cocked his head. "We don't know for certain that the threat is real, or how extreme it is. Elric has been king but for a year, and it's possible he's letting himself be scared by shadows. I want you to connect with the Tahlari tribe after you speak with the royal family. If there is dark magic in the area, they will be a better source of information. They were the key victims of Vairtross, they will know if this threat is real."

Lena shook her head at her father. "Of course it's real, Father! Why would the Kroll family lie about people being kidnapped? Why would they lie about their son being confronted with dark magic? What would they have to gain?"

Umbra could see that his daughter looked so young standing there. So out of her league in all of this. That was the precise reason he believed she should go. "It is my thinking that Elric is wishing to reconnect with me and reassure our alliance is still strong by giving me a fool's errand, to be honest. If I show up and defeat a minor threat for him, I will feel important to their mission, and then he can further use me in the civil war that's to come. All of this isn't a bad idea, but I cannot be taken away right now. I believe we can still achieve the perception of this alliance in this new king's rule by sending you."

Lena swallowed hard. He knew that he often put undue pressure on his daughter, but pressure is how you got pearls after all. Pressure, and an insane amount of time.

"No," she said simply, her face defiant.

"Excuse me?" Umbra boomed, standing up from his chair, his palms flat on his desk and squaring off with his daughter. Umbra stifled a laugh as he saw Amazadan take a step back towards the door as if he wanted to leave the uncomfortable scene.

"No," she repeated. Without another word, she turned and walked towards the door. Amazadan quickly glanced at Umbra for orders, but he just shrugged. Amazadan stepped aside and let Lena exit the office.

His friend approached the desk again, a half-smile on his face. "Shall I be going to Mt. Fluore then, My Lord?" he asked with a chuckle, but half expecting his king to say yes.

Umbra shook his head. "She'll come around," he said, and then thought about how pig-headed his magically frustrated daughter could be. "Probably," he added with a scoff.

CHAPTER SIX

LIGHT VISION

Checking the structural soundness of the limb above her, Lena decided it looked sturdy enough, and climbed up onto it in one fluid movement from the trunk of the tree. She was now up high enough and concealed behind the tree leaves so she could hide from her prey.

The armored tallcutta had made a delicious meal the other day, but she wasn't hunting for food now. She was aiming to kill as many coyotes as she could to help thin their population. There had been some dead hens found in the academy's chicken coop recently, and Lena could tell it was the work of a coyote.

Of course, her father's answer was to put up a beast repellent spell. The problem with that was that no one ever remembered to renew the spell, and it only lasted a week. Without fixing the root of the problem, the booming coyote population, her father was just inviting more deaths of innocent hens, and a drying up of a staple of the academy food supply.

Peering down from her branch hideaway, Lena shook her head at her father's antics. Magic always had to be the answer to everything. Not only that, but using magic to be the savior of the country was also a requirement. She always wished she hadn't succumbed to the pressure of her father to join the academy and study Solana's Light.

Instead, she wished she had followed the path of her sister Sable and studied non-magical healing. It was better suited to her strengths. The problem was that after her oldest brother, Eldryn, had joined the Academy and his next two children chose different paths, Lena had a tremendous expectation to follow in her father's footsteps where the other two did not. Not having at least half his children follow him into The Light would show the elf king to be a failure. At least that's how her father saw it.

There was a rustling down on the ground, and Lena steadied herself in her crouch on the tree bough, pulling up her bow and readying her shot. Looking straight down her arrow, she could see the bushes in the distance shaking. Her finger twitched slightly in anticipation of letting the arrow fly to hit its mark. The bushes broke apart, and she almost loosed the arrow when she noticed it wasn't an animal at all, but an elf. Deciding it was probably a bad idea to shoot her fiancé, she let the bow go slack and threw it over her shoulder, tossing her arrow back in its quiver with the others.

Since there was no point in pretending that any animal within a hundred-yard radius wasn't scared away by the bumbling elf, Lena jumped down from the bough to greet him.

"Moryan. I almost shot you," she called out with a smile.

The tall, slender elf clad in fine green robes threw his hands wide, as if offended. "I know you aren't overly fond of me yet, Lena, but do I really look like such a beast to you?" he laughed.

It was true. Their marriage was an arranged one, and Lena had made clear her disdain over the whole situation. Not that Moryan wasn't a handsome elf, but the fact Lena hadn't been given a choice, and much like everything else in her life, her father was using her to further his own image. Moryan belonged to a well-to-do lord of Zelira, and marrying his daughter to a lord's son helped him ensure he always had the proper support on the Elven council.

"Not so much that you look like a beast," she jested, "but you amble about like a bumbling bull, and honestly you wore green into a forest where you knew the best hunter in the land was seeking prey. I can't say too much about your grace or smarts right now."

There was an awkward pause before Moryan spoke again. "I'm not too sure about my smarts right now either, because..."

"...because my father sent you to talk me into going on this mission, and you came anyway, knowing full well I wouldn't respond well to your prompting me to go either?" Lena asked, cutting him off in her typical flatline voice.

Moryan nodded. "My father told me to do whatever Umbra says while I'm here, so please pretend like I tried really hard to convince you when we go back to the academy, please."

Lena smiled at him. He was such a typical elf. Worried about the bureaucracy of it all and where he stood in the ranks. Besides the fact that it was an arranged marriage, it was another thing that Lena disliked about Moryan. He was just another male playing the power game. The fact that she wouldn't have chosen him outside the arrangement made it all the worse to think about.

Without warning, there was rustling in the bushes behind Moryan. He didn't even seem to notice as he stood there with his stupid grin, trying to get her to play politics for him. She quickly raised her bow and pointed it just over his left shoulder. Not being a hunter, he couldn't tell she wasn't aiming at him, and his eyes went wide.

"Hey!" he snapped, genuine fear etched across his face. "You can't..."

She released the arrow before he even had time to wince. It sailed a foot over his right shoulder, and the coyote that was stalking him let out a brief yelp before it slumped to the ground, dead. Lena ignored Moryan who was still standing stock-still in fear.

"You must have gotten too close to her pups on the way in," said Lena as she bent down to examine her shot. It was a clean shot right through the neck. "They don't normally attack elves like this."

Moryan turned to look at her, so scared from the incident he didn't realize that his hands were still hanging in the air in shock. He looked angry, but Lena didn't care. Maybe he would be so mad he'd go back to his father and call off the engagement. This thought brought her joy, but only momentarily as she realized that would never happen. Her father was too powerful to turn down a marriage into the royal chain of command.

"Right," he said, putting his hands down to dust off his robes, as if coming close to any kind of danger had dirtied them. His look of anger quickly turned to one of being impressed as he saw the clean kill she had just made. He looked up at Lena and saw her look of satisfaction at the kill. "What if I convince him to let you bring your bow?"

Lena just laughed. "That will never happen. He doesn't want to be embarrassed to have another royal family see his own offspring need a bow instead of being masters of magic."

"Well, I have to tell your father something," said Moryan, sounding a little annoyed.

"Easy," Lena shrugged, then hoisted the coyote over her shoulder to take back to the academy. "Tell him the answer is still no. He can go and meet the Krollians if it's so important to him." At that, she walked past Moryan and back towards the academy.

The male elf scrunched his face in disgust as she passed. "And what are you taking that thing with you for?"

"Makes good winter coats," she hollered back over her shoulder. "I make a good chunk of money selling coats and other handmade things," she said, and then added quietly to herself, "because the only thing people around here can actually make with their hands is little balls of light."

The candlelight flickered in the office, casting eerie shadows along the walls. The desk chair sat empty beside the desk. A gentle hum filled the air as Umbra sat on the ground, cross-legged, eyes closed, trying to make a connection. This wasn't how Solana normally talked to Umbra when he blessed him with a vision. It was never something he could do on request. The visions just hit him at the most inopportune times. But Umbra was getting desperate. He sat there at a crossroads between whether he should go on this journey in

Lena's stead, and what his role was in the eventual downfall of the Kroll family. What he needed now was guidance as to which way to go.

It was at Lena's one-hundred-and-thirtieth birthday celebration five years prior that he had his vision from Solana about the downfall of the Kroll family. Not only that, but in the vision a terrible plague had struck the land, and much of the populace would die. Umbra had been seeking guidance from Solana ever since, but it had been silent, like a deep, dark cave. Even less silent than that, because where caves usually had the sound of dripping water, he wasn't even getting a trickle from Solana. He was left with just a worrisome vision, and no guidance forward.

After a few more minutes dwelling on the silence, Umbra scoffed in frustration and flicked his hand. A small magical wind came from his fingertips and circled the room, blowing out all the candles around him and leaving him in complete darkness. He always prided himself on his visions from Solana, on his connection to their god. But now, sitting in the dark, Umbra felt like an abandoned child with no clear, guided path forward.

The wool blankets shifted and fell to the floor as Lena tossed and turned in the canopy bed in her dormitory. She'd been having a tough time getting to sleep, and now that she had finally drifted off, she soon wished she was awake again.

She was surrounded by water. Eerie purple light was coming up from the liquid as it rippled around her. She was walking through the water, but somehow she didn't feel any wet sensations along her skin. Cold, piercing eyes met her gaze, and she found herself walking towards a slender man. As she got closer, she could just make out in the dim light that he had a tall, jutting nose, and a giant smile. The man was laughing at her.

When she got close enough, the man's hand quickly lurched forward and grabbed her by the face. She could make out tattoos of dogs, hellhounds more like, running up the man's arms. The purple glow of the water was reflected in the man's eyes as he stared deep into hers. He never stopped laughing.

She tried to scream, but no sound came out, as suddenly the man's grip on her face tightened and he forced her head under the water. The water felt warm. Her initial reaction was to struggle against him, but somehow she felt calm. The purple water turned bright white, and she knew there was no need to struggle.

Coming out of the bright light, a man slowly took shape. Very different from the man she had just seen, this man had a kind face and radiant white robes. His skin didn't even carry a blemish, and he seemed to glow as he approached her through the light. His brown hair rippled down the side of his head and down past his shoulders, his face thin, like the man holding her in the water, but much more friendly.

"You must go," the man said. Lena was expecting a deeper voice, but it was of a normal mid-tone.

"Go where?" she asked.

"Your mission awaits," said the man. "And once it is done, you must bury and build."

Bury and build? What did that even mean? It was such an odd phrase, and Lena couldn't even begin to comprehend what this man was talking about. She stared at him, trying to place him. He somehow looked familiar. His words were soothing, and though she was drowning underwater, she felt extreme comfort in hearing his voice.

More light parted from behind the man, and the Academy of Solana appeared behind him. Lena tilted her head and watched in amazement as the man smiled and floated backwards. In the middle of the courtyard, the man floated until he joined with the statue of Solana that stood there, reaching for the sky, water pouring out from his upstretched hand. He melded completely into the statue, and Lena awoke with a start.

The phrase 'bury and build' echoed audibly around her as she sat straight up in bed, sweat inching its way down her forehead. She wiped the back of her hand across her brow and stared quizzically at the glistening sweat there, confused. Was that a dream, or had she just experienced her first vision from the god, Solana?

Later that same evening, Lena found herself in the kitchens packing her satchel with provisions for her trip to Mt. Fluore. Her father had been elated at her change of mind, though she hadn't dared to tell him about her vision from Solana. Instead, she had told him that Moryan's speech in the woods had gotten through to her, and she had never seen the man smile any wider than he had at that moment.

She wasn't sure why she hadn't told him about the vision. In all honesty, he probably would have been elated that she had been spoken to by the god, that this was some sign in her hope for great magical abilities in the future, even if it was just as a visionary. It was a weird feeling in the pit of her stomach that told her to lie, though. Something told her that her father wouldn't react the way she had thought he would. That he would somehow resent her for her connection with the god, when it was well known within the family that he was still trying to figure out his last vision from Solana five years prior.

So now she was packing up dried tallcutta and rye bread for her mission to the mountains. It was the last thing she had to do before she set off. Her father had forbidden her to take her bow and arrows with her, which had riled her up to no end. He wanted a show of magical force on this mission, as that's the value that the Kroll family saw in their alliance. Showing up with rudimentary weapons would make them look weak. At least that's how Umbra had posited it during their brief chat.

Wedging one last slice of bread into the last spot in the satchel, mostly to better hide something at the bottom, she flipped the cover shut and slung it over her shoulder, turning to leave. She could not, however, as a figure stood in the doorway of the exit. Startled, she placed a hand on her chest and let out a sigh.

"Oh, my... I didn't know you were so good at sneaking up on people!" she exclaimed. She was almost impressed at how quietly he had approached. Maybe there was a good tracker deep down inside him somewhere.

Moryan smirked at her as he sauntered over. "Just wanted to stop by and say thanks for telling your father I had any impact at all on your decision to go." He paused, waiting for her to fill the silence. When she didn't, he added, "So... what made you decide to go?"

She stared up into his blue eyes, looking for signs of bad intentions. Deciding he was being genuine, she told him about her vision. He was going to be her husband after all. She'd have to learn to confide in him at some point. Plus, it was a good test to see if what she told him got back to her father. It was an exercise in trust.

When she finished telling him, he whistled a high note. "Apparently you've got your father's gift," he said, amazed. After she gave him a blank stare for a moment, he said, "Don't worry, Lena. I will not tell him. Frankly, I feel like it might break him if he knew." He smiled at her, and she felt her stomach flutter for just a moment.

"Given the fact that Solana is involved," Moryan continued, "don't you think this mission is a little more dangerous than you previously thought? Maybe your father should go instead of you."

She cracked a half-smile and reached up around to grab the back of his neck. Even though she was taller than most female elves, he was still a full head taller than her. She pulled his head down to her level and gave him a small peck on the cheek. "I appreciate you being worried about me, but I'll be fine. Why do you think my father is sending me? He knows it's a visit in good faith. The Kroll family is new to ruling. The new king is just a bit jumpy. Everything will be fine."

Moryan nodded, knowing he could never change her mind on something once it was set, no matter how hard he tried. Lena gave him a pat on the shoulder and started for the door. She grabbed the doorframe and turned to say one more thing that was on her mind. "Just keep an eye on my father while I'm gone, please."

He nodded again and watched her disappear out of the kitchen. He had a good feeling he would see her again, but something in his gut told him she wouldn't be the same person when she came back. Even if she was, there was a gap between them that would never be resolved so they could create a comfortable marriage. He knew she was too independent to be tied down.

CHAPTER SEVEN

AMONG THE TAHLARI

T he shadow of the mountains fell over the pine forest. It was odd being so dark at this time of day because it was only just past midday. The shade brought a chill breeze through the woods, but Lena didn't mind as she sat by the campfire she had made.

True, it was too early to stop for the night, but since her father had forbidden her from bringing her bow and arrow with her, she decided to take some time to make a new one for this mission. She didn't think she'd need it, but she didn't really care how it made her or her father look using 'rudimentary weapons'. She would rather be able to functionally help if need be, and to do that she needed her bow and arrows.

Over the last several days of her journey, she had been collecting the pieces she needed to create her new weapon. Branches of dogwood trees would work well for her bow and the arrow shafts. She'd been collecting turkey feathers she saw along the way as well. Her pockets were full of obsidian from the shores of Lake Carana. The only thing she had sneaked out from under her father's watchful gaze as she left was the quiver that she had folded down neatly and stuffed into the bottom of her provision bag, hidden well under bread and meat.

Now that she had most of the pieces she needed, she sat by the fire with the charcoal she'd obtained from her fires of the past few nights, and sap from the pine trees that now surrounded her. She was heating these two ingredients into a glue that she could use to piece together her arrows. The nettle fibres she'd collected could be woven together to make the bowstring. The fibres also worked well for tying the feathers and arrowheads to the arrow shafts.

It was a long and arduous process, but it made her happy every time she was crafting. Having spent her time the last few nights of travel whittling and prepping the materials, everything was coming together quickly now that her glue was ready. Her mind was totally free as she assembled the pieces, first the bow, and then six arrows that fit nicely into her quiver.

The hours passed effortlessly, and Lena almost forgot about the anxiety she had been feeling heading in to talk to the new rulers of the mountains. Barely a young adult elf now, she had been nothing more than a child when her father had helped the Kroll family destroy the dark kingdom. It was a lot to live up to, but having her weapon of choice would make it much easier to palate.

It didn't seem long before full-on darkness enveloped her as she was finishing the last few arrows. As she fit her dozen new arrows nicely into the quiver, she heard a rustling in the bushes. Without a second thought, she snatched an arrow nimbly from the quiver and strung it in her new bow. Unfortunately, she hadn't had the time to take test shots and break the bow in, but on first pull it felt nice in her grip.

Expecting some kind of animal predator sneaking up on her, she was shocked to see a human head pop up from the bushes. First one, and then several. Before she could decide whether or not they were friendly, she heard leaves rustling all around her, and she realized she was surrounded.

Her fire was casting an eerie glare on their painted faces. She could see bursts of color radiating out from their noses, a spot on each of their cheeks, and one on their chin. Squinting through the darkness, she could just make out the symbols. Suns. One large one in the center of their face across the nose, and three smaller suns surrounding this. The sign of Solana.

Lena slowly loosened her grip and pointed the slack arrow down at the ground. She wondered how long these people had been watching her. Given their appearance, they were primitive and did not belong to any specific kingdom. While she was great at hiding and sneaking up on prey compared to those back at the Academy of Light, these people lived in the woods, and she admitted they had easily gotten the drop on her without her knowing. It was an eye-opening truth.

Slowly, she put the arrow back in her quiver and slung her bow across her back, the string resting across her torso to keep the bow from falling. She raised her hands in the air as the men and women around her stepped closer.

"Hello," Lena said, hoping they spoke native and could understand her.

An older woman with a flat nose and graying hair stepped forward. She was wearing a fantastical lavender dress that flowed down to her ankles. She made Lena feel underdressed in her off-white hooded traveling cloak.

"Hello," the older tribeswoman said. "We had heard an elf was coming to help..." there was a pause as the woman sized her up. "We were expecting Umbra."

Lena fought hard not to roll her eyes. Even the primitives in the woods knew of her father and his reputation as savior against the dark. It seemed that even on a mission that her father had given to her, she wouldn't be able to escape his shadow.

She planted a smile on her face before she responded. "My father is busy with another important matter. I've been sent in his stead."

The old lady looked back at another tribesman, who shrugged. The lady turned back to Lena. "You must follow us then. Dallin ed' Suna would like a word."

Turning her head and looking at the woman from the side, Lena wasn't sure what to make of this statement. "No, I can't. My mission is to talk with the Kroll family about..."

"... about the dark ritual the Kroll family has witnessed? Yes, we know. We know much better than they do. Dallin has information about this cult that you will want to hear."

The word caught Lena off-guard. Cult? She had expected that the Kroll family were just being paranoid, and that a few bad actors were causing trouble. But an organized cult?

"Yeah, okay. I'll follow you," she said. Her mission was to speak to the Krollians first, but the Tahlari had decided that they wanted the lead.

The old woman nodded, and the others in the tribe fell in around Lena after she'd gathered her things and put out her fire. She and the others then followed the old lady as she led them back through the pine forest. For being a group of around fifteen people, Lena noticed how silent everyone was as they moved. It was so quiet that she could hear the call of an owl not too far off. She wasn't sure why, but she felt comfortable around the tribespeople. Back home, no one cared so much about stealth and just ambled about as they walked. Here, she could tell she was among people who loved and respected nature as she did.

Before long, the forest gave way to a worn footpath, and then buildings in the distance. As they approached, Lena could see that they were huts made of logs, chopped down and hewn from the pine trees surrounding them. The roofs of the huts appeared to be made from dried prairie grass gathered from outside the forest. Small children were chasing each other around the huts, tossing a ball made from an animal bladder back and forth.

Older tribespeople could be seen sitting around outside the huts, whittling wood, cooking on fires, and weaving together thick grasses to make baskets.

Lena smiled as she made her way through the small village. It was a pleasant change of pace to see things actually being made by hand instead of bought and imported. The path of houses led up to a large circular area of bare ground. Different-sized buildings filled this area, including a much wider building on the edge of the circle opposite the walking path they had just come down. This was clearly the center of the village, that was a frequented common area.

The old lady she had been following motioned her towards the large building in the center. As Lena stepped through the doorway, her awe at the robustness of the primitive village only grew. The building was twice as tall as any of the surrounding huts, and the floor she now stood on was made of the same pine wood, but the logs were cut in half and flipped to provide a flat walking surface. The floors in both her home kingdom of Zelira and The Academy of Light were either made of stone or magically processed wooden planks, so the craftsmanship here was ingenious to her.

Seated at the back of the room was a semicircle of people. They bore the same tattoos as those who had led her here. These individuals appeared to be much older than the other adults out in the village. As Lena made her way back to this new group, her eyes focused on the heavier-set old man in the middle of the semicircle. He wore a crown of leaves on his head that was almost comically tall. Lena gave a slight nod as she approached, not sure if she should bow.

The old man raised his hand and gestured at the ground opposite him, and Lena took a seat on the ground where he had gestured. There was a thin mat laid there that made sitting on the ground a little more bearable, and she sat waiting for the man to speak. When he did, it was in a language she couldn't understand. The woman to his right was nodding along as he spoke, and when he finished, the woman turned to speak to Lena in native so she could understand.

"Chief Dallin ed' Suna gives his greetings and warm welcome. He also says that it was expected that King Umbra of Zelira was going to come to aid the Kroll family."

Lena pursed his lips momentarily and then decided it was best to be friendly. Her face broke into a smile as she spoke to the woman. "Umbra is my father. He is very busy on another assignment, but has the utmost confidence in my ability to handle this situation." Even as she spoke the words, she felt a pang of shame, knowing they likely weren't totally true.

After translating this back to the chief, he nodded in understanding, staring at her with squinted eyes. After a moment, Lena felt a sense of relief as the chief nodded. "Chief Dallin has sensed that Umbra is wise in this decision. He welcomes you and your assistance in this matter," the translator said.

Lena cocked her head in confusion. "My help in this matter? This matter was called to our attention by the Kroll family."

A moment of translation got her an answer. "The Kroll family may have called you here, but we are more involved than them. The Tahlari people are the ones being kidnapped. Taken from our village by force in the night. Three from the Kroll family go missing, and all the sudden it is their concern. We have lost almost a hundred of our people across the clans, all young men."

Eyes wide, Lena tried to conceal her shock, but she knew she was doing a poor job of it. "I'm sorry? Did you say one-hundred people have gone missing?" This wasn't just a case of a few men from the Kroll family being lost. This was a large-scale epidemic of raiding and kidnapping.

The translator nodded, not needing the chief to speak this time in order to answer. "All men. Mostly young men. The chief's son was among the last group that was taken. Horns wail in the night. Panic spreads through the village as we try to hide the young men. Torches surround us, and before we know it, our village is being raided by large men in masks with the faces of serpents. Any who resists and tries to protect the young men is beaten down. The young men are drugged and taken away."

Lena noticed she was running her fingers along her bowstring that was pressed against her chest. Somehow, it helped to calm her a bit. She had expected this to be a quick mission of tracking down a few Kroll men who had gotten lost in the woods or in a cave. Now she became nervous as she realized the scope of what she was dealing with.

"Any idea who is behind all this?"

The interpreter and the chief glanced at each other before the chief nodded and gestured for the interpreter to elaborate. "Karkathi ed' Sayana," the woman said. Lena shrugged and shook her head, not recognizing the name. "Your father met him before when he helped us take down the Kingdom of Vairtross. He likely wouldn't remember him though," the woman paused and glanced at the chief again. Another nod, and she said, "in a sense, he is Chief Dallin's oldest son."

Now the chief spoke continuously as he told his story, pausing only for the interpreter to catch up to his words. She said, "Long ago, the Tahlari were slaves to the Firestar family in Northern Darmark. We were worked hard in the blistering sun, beaten and whipped, forced to build an empire for the Firestar family rule. It was because of these conditions that the Kroll family waged war against the Firestars and freed us from their oppression."

Lena was shocked by this information. She had heard a few tales of the country Darmark to the south, but she hadn't heard about the Kroll family's deeds in freeing the Tahlari. She was beginning to get a picture of why they were so revered.

"While the Kroll family were our saviors, they were also overly-righteous in their deeds, and wanted to stomp out the Firestar family from existence. Every last one of them. That included the son of Walther Firestar. At the time, Karkathi was only six years of age, and his name was Werner. Werner fled the massacre of his family and wound up in the den of Tahlari slaves. Dallin was not yet our chief at that time, and knew that Werner was the son of our enemy, but even so, looking into the eyes of that scared, six-year-old-boy, he could not let the Kroll family harm him."

"Vaaron Kroll and his men tracked Werner to the den of the slaves, but when Vaaron questioned us if we had seen the boy, Dallin squared off against the would-be king, and told him that the boy had been there, but had run off into the mountains. Dallin saved the boy's life that day and took him in as one of us. Werner became Karkathi ed' Sayana, Child of the Lost." Both the chief and the woman stopped talking, allowing Lena to process it all.

After a moment, Lena realized she was expected to reply. "Why would Karkathi be kidnapping boys from the village when you all took him in and saved his life? Who would bite the hand that feeds them?"

The old chief sighed, a tear rolling down his cheek. He spoke again, and the interpreter said, "Karkathi had long talked of revenge on the Kroll family for what they did to his father. Dallin had always preached peace and forgiveness to him, but Karkathi had a vendetta ingrained in his soul since that fateful day. A few months ago, Karkathi disappeared. The raids started shortly after. Before he left, he said he had contacted someone who knew his pain. Someone who could help him. Dallin urged him to stay, but one night, he was just gone."

Lena sighed. "So, where does that leave me? Why are you telling me all this before I go and see the Kroll family? I was called here by them, not you. But you've obviously intercepted me for a reason."

The interpreter nodded. "The Kroll family does not know that Werner even lives. They had assumed, since the boy was so young, that he had run off and died in the mountains. They don't know what they're up against here."

"And what are they up against?" Lena asked. "A madman with a lifelong vendetta? I'm sure they've dealt with worse."

The interpreter shook her head. "Karkathi spoke a bit of the man he contacted. The man who said he could help him exact his revenge. A man of magic."

Lena bit her lower lip. Her hand gripped her bowstring hard. She had come expecting to lead a search party. Instead, what she was being pulled into was a full-scale magic fight. "What kind of magic?"

Now it was the chief who spoke. It was just one word, but that word sent a frightening chill up Lena's spine. "Baladan."

CHAPTER EIGHT

KROLL RISING

The stalactites overhead were dripping down into the pool of purple water as Karkathi walked around the edge. He bit the long fingernail of his forefinger as he circled the pool, contemplating all the power that lay there waiting to be tapped.

It was a gift. A glorious, powerful gift from the dark god Baladan. Of course, Baladan was currently trapped away in another realm where Solana had contained his powers, but he had left traces of his power behind. Traces for others to use for their own dark intentions. For their own use, and Karkathi could only guess, to use on the quest to free him. Karkathi had ulterior motives in freeing the dark god, however. Having grown up to watch his family murdered, and then being forced to live in poverty had left him powerless his whole life. He was done with being powerless. Baladan was power.

With the power the pool provided, along with the aid of Malak, the old shaman, and his army of Dark Humans, he could finally take his revenge on those who had murdered his family: the Krollians. Once he had wiped out every last one of them, he would be in a much better position to march south and retake Darmark in the name of the Firestars.

The plan was already in motion. Around a month ago, he and Malak had successfully killed the man who had murdered his father, Vaaron Kroll. To cover their tracks, they had made it appear to be a hunting accident, leaving his son in charge. Elric was weak, indecisive, and raw from the loss of his father. This weakening of the Kroll family, paired with his new army, was creating the perfect scenario to exact his revenge.

Karkathi's colorful robe snagged a rock, and he pulled it free. As he did so, he glanced at the tattoos that ran down his arms. He hated them so. They were given to him by the man who took him in, Dallin. He could never bring himself to call the man his father. Walther was his father, and had been murdered by those pious fools who thought themselves better than the Firestars. The tattoos, he was told, were to help him blend in with the Tahlari tribe and not raise suspicions about who he really was. Symbols of the god, Solana. Depictions of Tahlari history. All part of the ruse, the fake life that Karkathi had to portray just to survive the murderous hands of the Krollians.

Speaking of the Krollians, Karkathi had now made his way to the back of the cave where three of them still lay, having been murdered by one of his Dark Humans several days prior during their last ritual. Malak had cast a preservation spell on them so their bodies still appeared as though they had been freshly killed. He smiled as he looked down at them.

They were men he recognized from his frequent spying from the shadows. One of them he knew as Rangston, son of Falton, brother to the new king. Next to him lie Baron and Bucklow, sons of Jarina, the sister. He was shocked at the good fortune that had come during the ritual. Not only had their conversion of Tahlari youth into Dark Humans been a success, but he had also dealt another blow to the Kroll family by taking out a few of their heirs.

Something bit at this thought. One of them had escaped. The one he had recognized as Reeve Kroll. The golden child. They had been unable to find him, and it was likely that the cult's presence was now known. Not that it mattered. The plan was in motion, and could not be stopped. A few more batches of converted Tahlari, hopefully some successful experimenting with the dwarves, and he would have enough men under his command to arm them and take the mountain from the inside.

"Admiring our prized victims?" said a voice in the pale light of the pool. Karkathi looked up to see Malak had finally joined him. The dark-skinned sorcerer was wearing his usual snake-head crown, a symbol of his lost status as the shaman of Vairtross. Like Karkathi, Malak had lost everything because of the Kroll family. Ever weak, the Krollians had summoned elves of light magic to come and destroy the Virmorphia users of Vairtross, razing the entire kingdom to the ground. Once destroyed, the Krollians had stuck the Tahlari where the kingdom had once stood. Only Malak and a few dozen others had managed to escape the carnage alive. Just more survivors of the cruelty of the Kroll.

"Just reveling in what they are about to become," he answered the old shaman.

Malak grinned and nodded. He had been waiting decades for this moment. The moment he could exact his revenge. In exile, after many decades in the shadows, Malak had been given a vision from Baladan. A vision that a Tahlari man was also seeking the same vengeance. He had sent his brute enforcer to contact Karkathi, and Karkathi had gone to rally Malak and the other scattered exiles of the Vairtross cult.

Raising his wrinkled hands, Malak began to chant the words in an old, forgotten language. Purple light formed between his arched fingers, converging above his palm into a single point of light. Once the light grew bright enough, or he reached a certain point in his spell, Karkathi couldn't tell which, Malak raised his hand towards the dead Krollians sprawled out on the cave floor.

Like lightning across the sky, the beam shot from Malak's hand and hit each of the dead in turn. Karkathi stared in awe as the bodies writhed, the electric jolt coursing through their bodies.

Even though he knew what the end goal was, the sight of the bodies moving still sent an icy chill up his spine. And then, the eyes of Rangston popped open just as the chill reached his neck, and Karkathi's eyes grew wide. Having seen the creation of Dark Humans was nothing compared to seeing the dead brought back to life.

"Rise!" yelled Malak in native, and the dead men snapped right up to attention in such a way that a live person could not. They stared blankly at the pair of men in colorful robes, waiting for their next command.

Karkathi smiled. Not only was the Kroll family weak, but they now had some key members working directly for him.

"Where are we?" the one Karkathi recognized as Bucklow asked.

"The cave where you died," said Karkathi curtly. "The cave where you have been reborn. Also, the cave where you will help us create more Dark Humans until we've amassed an army big enough to storm Mt. Fluore and kill every last Kroll there."

The three men's eyes all bulged in horror, and all Karkathi could do was laugh as there was nothing they could do to disobey.

CHAPTER NINE

REEVE

B ooming voices could be heard on the other side of the large oak doors, and Lena paused to gather herself. She had slept well enough in the village the night before, one lovely couple offering their home for her to sleep. She had initially refused their gesture, not wanting to impose, but they had been very insistent, becoming offended she was denying their offer.

It wasn't a lack of sleep that was making her nervous now. It wasn't even the loud voices on the other side of the door as she listened to the Kroll family arguing fervently about something. It was the conversation she'd had with Chief Dallin that was still ringing through her mind.

Growing up watching her father and brother use Solana's Light, and then going on to fail miserably at it herself, made it painfully clear that Solana was real. She had never questioned that. Given that he was real, it would then make sense that his counterpart, Baladan was real as well. It had just never cropped up in her life in such a real sense as hearing people were actively using his dark magic. Now she was here to help hunt them down and put a stop to it.

She pulled at the cloak where it hugged her neck, resisting the urge to throw the hood up and hide away. The robe had been white when she'd left the academy, but was now a lavender color and smelled of flowers. The same couple that had given her their home for the night had also taken her robe, satchel, and bow as she dined with the tribe. Chief Dallin's translator had told her they would keep her things safe in their lodging. When she had gone to the hut after dinner, her things were waiting for her, but her robe was now soaking in a bucket. When she awoke that morning, the couple had dried it for her, and it was now violet.

She thought it an odd gesture, but accepted it from the couple and thanked them multiple times for their generous accommodations.

Now, placing her hand on the handle of the giant door, she wondered if the flower smell would make her seem weak. Heaving a deep sigh, she decided there was nothing else for it. She grabbed the handle and threw the door wide.

She was greeted by an ornate room with a long wooden table down the center. Surrounding the table were tall, decorative chairs, though no one in the room was sitting down. Instead, they were all standing and pointing at each other as if they had been in the middle of a large debate and were blaming each other for all their recent misfortunes.

The room went more silent than night in the woods, and every eye was suddenly on her as she strode awkwardly through the threshold. Most of the people in the room appeared to be older, though two young men stood at the far end of the table. One appeared to be close to her age, though she knew she was older than everyone here, given the fact that they were all humans.

Not sure if she should bow and greet them as royalty, also being royalty herself, she settled with a slight hand raise and a head nod as she said, "Hello, I'm Princess Lena of Zelira. My father has sent me to consult with you about your problems."

There was a long silence as everyone stared at her with increasingly narrow eyes. The man at the far end of the table with the crown, presumably King Elric, whispered something hurriedly out of the corner of his mouth to the older man on his right. This man shrugged and whispered back, gesturing at the king and then over at Lena. She couldn't make out what they were saying, but she could guess it wasn't friendly.

Finally, after several more whispered exchanges, King Elric cleared his throat loudly, and put what he thought looked like a genuine smile on his face, though she could read something else there. "Welcome, Lena, we were...expecting King Umbra."

Lena tried to make her smile back feel more genuine than King Elric's looked, but she feared it likely looked just as fake. "My father sends his regrets that he is busy tending to other important matters." She paused for a moment, thinking about her father's objectives in sending her and why he didn't just ignore the matter or tell them they couldn't make it. "When the Kroll family sends a message of need, Zelira always wants to make sure it doesn't go ignored."

Elric nodded and gestured to a seat next to the two younger men in the room. "Thank you, Lena. Please have a seat here next to Reeve."

Lena made her way around the room, all eyes on her as she went. Halfway down the long table, she glanced out the window. The view of Zaroft from here was breathtaking. Morning light shone down on the shorter mountain peaks before here. Beyond that were the pine forest and then grasslands as far as the eye could see.

As Lena turned back towards the table, her eyes caught those of the one Elric had called Reeve, and her stomach did a somersault. He was standing, one hand on the back of the chair he had pulled out for her. His other hand gestured for her to sit. His smile seemed to be the only genuine thing in the room.

As she drew closer, she noticed how blue his eyes were, the same deep blue as Lake Carana. She felt her face flush as she realized she was staring. Moving quickly to sit before he realized her face was red, she set her satchel on the ground next to her chair and pulled herself in closer to the table.

As Reeve sat down next to her, she found herself looking out of the corner of her eye at him. His messy hair looked all out of sorts, but somehow still nice. Her stomach felt like it was in a knot, and she internally scolded herself. He was a human, likely over one-hundred years younger than her, though he looked developmentally the same. Regardless of how close in age they seemed biologically, she would still outlive him by many millennia.

Trying to push Reeve from her mind, but still painfully aware of his presence right next to her, Lena cleared her throat and looked expectantly towards the king, waiting for him to speak.

The king had a half-smile on his face, and she knew she'd been caught fawning. To her relief though, Elric became all business, and spoke to the pressing matters at hand. "So, Lena, your father has been a great help in the past, helping us defeat the kingdom of Vairtross. It seems we still have some remnants of dark magic lingering. Is this something you are equipped to help us with?" he asked, eyeing her hand that was absentmindedly playing with the bowstring strung across her chest. She immediately knew that his seeing such a mundane weapon made him think she wasn't the right person for this mission.

Being familiar with people looking down on her preference for the bow, she smiled and replied, "While it is true that I'm still a student, I have confidence in my abilities to handle anything for your great family." Maybe she should have taken part in the theater at the academy? She felt her portrayal of false confidence was going over well.

There was a scoff from across the table. Elric turned to glare at the man. "You'll have to excuse my brother," said Elric. "He is still grieving the loss of his son in recent days, and has apparently forgotten how manners work." Elric turned to look pointedly at his brother.

The golden-robed man across the table still glared at her, not caring that he had just been scolded by his king. His balding head shone above his wrinkled face. His mouth turned down into a scowl as he spoke to her, his voice not becoming any brighter.

"Three of our royal family have gone missing, dead by the accounts of Reeve, and we are sent a student to help us. Hardly a favor..."

"Hold your tongue!" Elric snapped at him. "Umbra has sent us aid, and we will use what help we can get. She said she is capable of helping, and we have no reason not to take her at her word."

The man slunk back down into his chair, silent but visibly fuming. Elric chose to ignore his brother's pouting and continue his conversation with Lena. "As I'm sure you've heard from your father, we've had three of our family disappear while investigating a disturbance reported by the Tahlari."

Before Lena could answer, Reeve cut her off. "It's likely that Lena knows more about all this than we think, Father. She's been with the Tahlari already."

Lena shot him a look. Elric glared at his son as well. It seemed like the king was having trouble keeping everyone in line. And Reeve? Had he been spying on her the previous night? She cocked her head and waited for him to explain, trying not to let his good looks block her suspicion.

Reeve cleared his throat nervously, a half-smile on his face as he spoke to her. "Purple clothing is common among the Tahlari. From the smell of lavender, your cloak is freshly dyed. I don't think you're a day late because you decided to stop and color your cloak."

Lena nodded. The prince had good intuition. He would make an excellent tracker on a hunt. The thought of hunting with him alone in the woods sent another flush feeling through her face, and she knew she must look very red. The king's brother shot Reeve an odd, knowing look and a half smile.

"He's right," she said. "They stopped me at my campsite last night, and a delightful couple let me have their hut. They are the ones who dyed my cloak."

"They must like you a lot," said Reeve. "They don't like to share their dye with just anyone."

Lena thought about it for a moment. "Not sure if it was about them liking me so much as them wanting me to know Karkathi's motives behind all this."

Chairs slid back from the table, and everyone's jaws dropped. A few of the older Krollians stood and placed their hands firmly on the table. The king's brother spoke.

"They told you who is behind all this? You know the animal who supposedly killed my son?"

Lena nodded. She proceeded to tell them everything that Chief Dallin and his translator had relayed to her the night before. The people in the room listened with rapt attention, and when she was done, Elric had to work to calm his brother down.

"Easy, Falton," he said, lowering his hand in a motion to tell his brother to lower his anger.

"Don't tell me to be easy, Brother. You and Father always defended the Tahlari as your big, noble cause. Your spy network. And here they are, hiding our oldest enemy. Tell me, Elric, what other secrets are they out there hiding from us? Maybe we should just let this Karkathi finish them all off and be done with it. Then we can focus on more important matters, like keeping Zaroft from devolving into a civil war!"

"I don't think Reeve here would be too happy if we let the Tahlari die out," said Rasgar from beside his brother. After the glare he got from his father, he realized he shouldn't have chimed in, and went quiet. Lena looked to Reeve and saw it was his turn for a flushed face.

"What does he mean by..." Lena started to ask, but Elric cut her off.

"We are not letting the Tahlari die off. We need to stop Karkathi and his use of dark magic before it grows and infects us all. The fate of the Tahlari is interlinked with ours. If they go extinct, we will not be too far behind."

Falton scoffed. "What do you propose we do then, Elric? Sending in what few troops we have won't do much against dark magic, and will just leave us defenseless."

The king stroked his beard in thought. "Based on Reeves' report, this cult was at the dark pool to perform a ritual. They were coming from the outside. This makes me think they don't have their base set up in this cave..."

"But the pool gives them power," Lena added.

"Precisely," said Elric, snapping his fingers and pointing at Lena. "The pool is their source of power. So we cut it off. I say we send a battalion of men down to secure the outside entrance to the cave. Then, Lena, would you be able to track down the cult and take out their leaders? Cut the head off this snake, and hopefully the rest of the cult will wither and die."

Heart skipping a beat, Lena swallowed hard. Was she ready to take on a magical cult? She supposed that a well-aimed arrow could take care of any type of creature if she hit the right spot, magic or not.

She nodded that she could help, knowing that her father wouldn't back down from any challenge, especially one that is indebted the Kroll family to them further if successful. Her father's visions told her that Zaroft would one day be totally ruled by the Kroll family. It was their job to help them fulfill that destiny.

Then the vision of Solana came crawling back to the front of her mind. "Of course I will help; that is why I'm here. Only... I do not know these mountains or these woods. I don't even know where the cult's cave is located. Where do I begin?"

Rasgar's face lit up. "I will go with you!" he said eagerly.

"Don't be silly, Brother," Reeve cut in. "You are the heir to the throne, and this mission is dangerous. I will accompany Lena." Reeve reached out and placed a hand on top of hers on the table. A tingle shot from her hand up her arm. He looked at her, but she avoided his gaze. He quickly realized this made things awkward and gave her hand a quick pat and turned back towards his father, waiting for his reaction.

The half-smile returned to Elric's face, and suddenly Lena wished she were anywhere else in Zaroft. She was on a mission, and here it was blatantly obvious that she was pining for this king's son.

Elric nodded. "Reeve, you can be Lena's guide..." Rasgar scoffed at being passed over on his offer so easily and tried hard to disappear into his chair. "...but I've almost lost you once. Heir or not, you are still very important to this family. You are to leave any direct conflict with this dark cult to Lena, do you understand me?"

Reeve nodded vigorously, and she could feel him looking excitedly towards her. Her face felt hot as she felt him looking at her, but she tried desperately to avoid eye contact.

"Where do we start then?" she asked, running a hand through her hair and tucking it behind her ear, staring at the table.

Reeve thought for a moment. "The dwarves in the mines helped us find the cave through the tunnels; maybe they have some insight into where the cult lives?"

"As good a place to start as any," said Lena. She had never seen a dwarf in real life before, only in childhood storybooks. In the stories, they were usually bumbling oafs and lessons to children about not being greedy. She assumed these stories had originated with a grain of truth from somewhere.

"Great! I will get provisions, and we will set out by this evening!" With that, Reeve kicked back his chair and hurriedly left the room. As he vacated his spot, Lena could see the still-fuming Rasgar sitting in his chair, arms folded and pouting. He looked very much like his uncle who sat across from him.

Lena turned to Elric and his knowing half-smile. Despite what the king was thinking, and no matter how attractive she found Reeve, it was an impossible infatuation that could go nowhere. She stood and bowed slightly, excusing herself to the hallway outside where she planned to put Reeve out of her mind and focus on the mission at hand, all the while thinking about where he went and that the next time she saw him they would be heading out together alone.

CHAPTER TEN

PETARO

The entrance to the mining tunnels was ominous and dark. The gaping cave entrance was carved into the mountainside, too smooth to have formed naturally. Lena looked up above the entrance and saw words carved into the stone arch that read 'Petaro Mining City'.

She had to admit, she was a bit nervous to meet dwarves. There weren't that many throughout Zaroft, and they had a reputation of being unfriendly to outsiders. From what she'd heard, they loved whatever business they were involved with, and made success and wealth their whole life. Anything else in the world was either meant to help them grow their business or was a hindrance. It was a stark contrast to the Elven society she was used to, where arts and magic flourished. Money was rarely needed back home, but when it was, there was plenty of it.

She felt a hand on her upper back, and a chill ran down her spine. Reeve had placed his hand there to help guide her forward, and she realized she had stopped and stared at the arch for an awkward amount of time.

"We should get a move on so we can find out our next move before nightfall," Reeve said in her ear. She jumped forward and continued walking, trying to think about their upcoming meeting with the dwarves, and not about how good Reeve looked in his fresh, blue tunic.

"I agree. I was just checking out the craftsmanship," she said as they entered the cave.

The first room they entered smelled of must. It was a damp cave smell Lena had only experienced a few times in her life. To their right was another carved-out section of the mountain sporting a long wooden table on a raised platform. Behind the table was a row of pickaxes hanging by leather straps. To the left, a mine cart sat on tracks that led into the obscurity of another dark tunnel. The only sound was the echoing of their footfalls on the stone ground.

"Doesn't look like anyone is here," said Lena. She wasn't expecting a grand entrance surrounded by miners, but the fact that no one was around, and not even a sound could be heard, was unsettling.

Reeve went over to the table by the pickaxes and looked back into the empty area. "Don't worry, they're always here. Mining is their life."

She let out a silent laugh at how right the stories had been about a dwarf's love of work. She wondered if they were totally selfish, like in the stories, too. "Still, I don't like it. This seems odd."

"Don't like it?" asked Reeve. "Well, then what would you like? A grand feast and a welcome as honored guests? Maybe they'll tap into the good ale for us." He laughed.

"No," said Lena while she examined the mine cart. "Some kind of contact would be good though. They obviously aren't working the mines in force. Only a few pickaxes are missing from that wall."

"Maybe they work at night?" said Reeve. "When I was here with my cousins, it was nighttime and most of the pickaxes were missing."

"Or maybe they've shut down operations to send out a search party," said a booming voice from the shadows. They both looked, and from around the corner up ahead came a dwarf. He was about half Lena's height, but what surprised her was the shock of bright red that made up the dwarf's hair and beard. His forehead was wrinkled with age, and his nose was crooked as if it had been broken at some point in his life.

Lena gawked at his clothing, never having seen anything like it before. He wore a thick wool undershirt, topped with a brown leather vest. He had brown leather pants to match, though she doubted he was trying to match for style. His arms sported leather bracers topped off with gloves. All protection for a hard day's work in dangerous conditions.

"You've got a lot of nerve coming here after what you did," he boomed at Reeve.

Reeve looked shocked and pointed at himself. "What I did? A search party? What happened here, Garrun?"

Garrun's eyes darted back and forth. Lena and Reese came in closer, sensing they were being watched as Garrun now looked scared.

"I've said too much already," the dwarf said. "They heard you come in. They've been here since they followed you back through the tunnels the other day, and now they've taken over the mine and are stealing our stock of subfluore."

Reeve moved closer to the dwarf, his voice barely audible. "I am so sorry, Garrun. I had no idea. Can they hear us here?"

Garrun shook his head. "There are some of them waiting up around the third bend to ambush you. They sent me to draw you in. Just up this first access shaft..."

Lena lurched forward and tackled Garrun to the ground just as an arrow blazing in purple light soared just over his head. "They aren't waiting! They're here!"

Reeve drew his sword and faced off against their foes. Looking down the rock corridor, he saw he was up against five cult members of those that could be seen. It was hard telling how many more were around the corner in hiding. They were all clad in their menacing snake masks, so it was impossible to see their faces, but what he could see was their bows with glowing purple arrows drawn and ready to fire.

Abandoning any idea of attacking, he sheathed his sword and ran over to help Lena and Garrun up, pulling them out of the way just in time as a volley of arrows hit the spot they had just been lying. Their momentum carried them over to the mine cart, which provided minimal cover for the three of them while their enemy advanced.

"How many of them are there?" Lena asked, freeing her bow from around herself and nocking an arrow in one swift movement.

"Five I could see," said Reeve, wishing he had a ranged weapon on him, but placing a hand on his sword in case they came close enough.

Lena popped up quickly above the cart and fired off an arrow. A scream was heard in the distance.

"Down to four," said Lena, stringing another arrow. "Can we make a run for the entrance?"

Another arrow with purple light whizzed overhead. It clattered against the rock wall behind them, and Lena popped up to send another shot down the tunnel. She found her target just as the remaining cult members released a volley her way. One arrow was coming right at her, and her shot misfired as she jerked to duck down out of the way. She heard her arrow miss and clang off the wall behind her target.

"I don't think a run for the entrance would be safe," Garrun said. "The cult took over the mine, but they also kidnapped some of our workers. Took them out there somewhere. They'll likely be back for more of us soon. Sent some scouts out after them, but not sure they'll be there to back our escape."

Lena frowned. "What about this mine cart? Is the tunnel downhill? Can it get us out of here?" She popped up and fired another arrow to keep their enemy at bay while they made a plan.

Garrun shook his head, but Lena didn't see this response as she fired and struck another cult member in the neck with an arrow. "No," he said to make sure she heard. "The access shaft goes uphill. Easier to let full carts slide back down. It's operated on a pulley system. One of us would have to stay behind to operate it, and would get shot down before the others got very far."

"How many arrows do you have left?" Reeve asked her, drawing his sword.

"Eight or nine," she answered, trying to count back to how many she had fired out of the dozen she'd made."

"Fire them fast!" he yelled as he swiveled around the side of the mine cart and charged at the remaining enemies.

Before she had time to process what he was going to do, he was gone. She didn't have any time to think or stop him, so she stood up and fired off two arrows as quickly as she could at the targets that were turning towards Reeve to help cover him.

One dropped, and the other she'd only hit in the shoulder. A non-lethal shot. She cursed herself and fired another. This one missed completely, but it didn't matter at this point. Reeve had already engaged the group, and Lena watched in awe as they drew short swords against him, but to no avail.

It was obvious that Reeve had had a lot of practice with a sword, if not full-on battle experience. He quickly ran the first two men through, and then faced off against the next two that rounded the corner. The reinforcements didn't matter, as he quickly dispatched them, sending them slinking to the ground.

"So much for the 'Reeve is a guide and shouldn't engage the enemy' order," she said to herself, thinking back to how King Elric wanted his son to stay out of the fray. She wondered if word would get back to her father about how she had allowed the king's son to join the fight.

Garrun chuckled next to her. "Ain't no way we're keeping Master Reeve out of the battle, Miss. He cares too much." Lena smiled at this, her guilt somewhat eased.

Once the last body had landed with a thud, Reeve turned back towards the other two. "I don't see anyone else here. We should be safe to move. Where does this tunnel go, Garrun?"

The dwarf came out from behind the mining cart and grabbed a short sword from one of the fallen cult members. "This is the main mine shaft straight through the mountain. It branches off into tunnels that lead to subfluore alcoves. The Tahlari cult was stationed around the sleeping quarters and ration stash."

"The Tahlari aren't a cult!" snapped Reeve.

Lena looked at him through the awkward silence that followed. He looked angry and was kicking at a loose rock on the cave floor. Apparently, Reeve was more concerned with his grandfather's legacy of protecting the Tahlari than his father was. Since Garrun looked shocked that he'd offended him, Lena decided to quickly change the subject.

"You actually sleep down here in the dark?" Lena asked as she salvaged her arrows from her fallen foes, blocking the human aspect from her mind and trying to pretend the bodies on the ground were just animals she'd hunted. Only one arrow had broken after it impacted the wall, so she was happy she could recover so many.

Garrun shrugged. "Only when we have to catch up on supply. Most of us live out in the ..."

Garrun was cut off by yelling from the entrance of the mine. A team of five dwarves was barreling towards them, waving their short arms in the air in warning.

The dwarf in front looked very young compared to Garrun. His hair was brown, and his skin was smooth, at least what could be seen of it around his bushy facial hair. He was clad in a green vest and brown trousers as if he meant to blend into the forest he was just running from. The others were dressed in similar earth tones, but appeared to be closer to Garrun's age.

The lead dwarf ran straight to Garrun, out of breath and hardly able to speak. Garrun put a hand on his shoulder, trying to steady him. "What, Dareth? What's wrong?"

Catching his breath, Dareth pointed back towards the light. "We found the others at the cult's camp. They're in cages. Being tortured. We were spotted and couldn't help them. They are coming!"

Lena's head whipped back towards the entrance, and sure enough, a ways off in the distance, she saw a group of figures heading towards the mine. "Do we fight?" she asked, also picking up a short sword as Garrun had done.

Garrun tossed his short sword from one hand to the other and then pointed down the mine shaft. "No, there are too many of them. I think we can lose them if we go into the mine."

"I thought you said there were more of them in the mine?" yelled Reeve.

"Yes, but we have more opportunity to fight on our own terms in there than outnumbered here in the open. Move!"

Lena took one more glance back at those approaching the mine and estimated twenty warriors were bearing down on them. She quickly picked up a second sword for good measure and ran off after Reeve and the six dwarves.

CHAPTER ELEVEN
THE BRUTE

The tunnel grew narrower and darker as they ran. Soon the only light was coming from brackets on the wall where yellow crystals were mounted.

"Subfluore as lights?" Lena asked as they ran. Everything back home and at the Academy was lit by magical fire. Her father wanted to distance himself from such worldly uses of light and power.

"Yes," Garrun panted, trying to keep his breath as he ran. "The Tahlari are trying to take it from us and sell it to hire mercenaries against the Kroll family."

"The Tahlari aren't trying to take anything!" Reeve snapped. "They would never..."

A loud scream sounded from behind them, and they turned to see one of the scout dwarves, his face contorted in pain, drop to his knees and then face plant onto the hard stone ground. Behind him, they could see cult members and possessed

Tahlari closing in fast, one holding up a bow that had taken down the scout.

"No!" yelled the dwarf called Dareth as he pulled two daggers from his hips and went charging back after the murderer.

Lena didn't have time to think as she also turned and ran to join Dareth in the fight. She pulled both swords up in an 'X' in front of her to block an incoming arrow and then charged into the fray of oncoming tribesmen. Suddenly she was transported back to the intense sparring sessions she'd had with her brother, Garrick, in the training arena back in Zelira. Over the years she'd become proficient in dual-wielding short staffs. The sword's weight felt different in her hand, but her style with them still felt familiar as she carved through the first few enemies.

Reeve was beside her in an instant, blocking high swings coming down on Dareth, and killing cult members who were flanking him. Lena could tell he knew she had her side of things handled as he and Dareth worked their side of the cramped tunnel.

Warm blood ran free as Lena felt a slash on her right arm. She yelped slightly at the sting of the blade, but pulled her sword sharply across the air, taking her attacker's head clean off. The tribesmen behind him took a hesitant step back at this, but Lena noticed his face twitch, as if in intense pain, and then anger and resolve replaced the pain and fear, and he charged forward at Lena.

She was taken aback by his facial contortions and wasn't prepared for the attack, just as Reeve spun around and ran the man through with his sword.

Dareth dispatched the last one, and as the man fell, they were left in the dimly lit tunnel with a pile of bodies on the floor. They all looked at each other in relief. After a moment, the adrenaline of battle wore off, and Lena grabbed her arm in pain.

Seeing the blood, Reeve didn't hesitate to rip off a strip of his tunic and offer to wrap it around her arm. Lena nodded and let him tie the makeshift bandage around her arm tightly. When he was done, he looked up from his work and right into her eyes. Everything else seemed to melt away.

A gruff voice interrupted them as Garrun was bent over the fallen enemies, examining them. "I know you don't want to think these men are Tahlari, Master Reeve, but the tattoos on these four say otherwise."

They looked down to see Garrun pointing at the tattoos on some of their arms. It was a large sun surrounded by three smaller suns.

Reeve shook his head. "I know they're Tahlari, Garrun, but you didn't go to the pool. These men are brainwashed, under a spell. They aren't acting of their own accord."

"He's right," Lena chimed in. "Just now one of them looked absolutely horrified, like he had realized for a moment what was actually going on. A second later his face twisted in pain and he was back on the attack. Someone is controlling these men."

Reeve looked down at the other men on the ground. They all wore masks that bore a resemblance to a snake. "These men here," he said, "they drown the Tahlari in the pool, and they come out under their control. The man who attacked me had just drowned in the pool. Somehow, that's the source of their control. That's why my father sent troops to the pool to secure it."

Garrun shook his head. "We can't worry about the pool right now. We have to free the other dwarves being held captive deep in the mine."

Placing a hand on the dwarf's shoulder, Reeve gave him a serious look. "We're pressed for time, Garrun. We just came here to get someone to guide us to the cult's camp so we can take out their leader and end all this."

Garrun glared at Reeve and pushed his hand off his shoulder. "Oh, sure. Take Dareth with you then."

"Thank..."

"...after you help free the others," Garrun said, staring right up into Reeve's eyes with a ferocity that went way above his stature. Lena glanced at Dareth, who shrugged his shoulders.

"That's not what we signed up for here," said Reeve.

"But it's what you will do if you want our help. You may not have meant to, but you're the one who led these monsters into our mines. If you expect me to put another one of our own in danger to help you clean up this mess, help me first."

Reeve looked back at Lena who nodded her approval. "I still think the best plan is to cut the head off the snake, but you're right. If your dwarves are in immediate danger, we should help you free them."

"Thank you, Master Reeve. Let's move."

It felt weird leaving the dwarf who had fallen in the fight, but Garrun quietly reassured them he would send others to retrieve the body for a proper burial later. Now they had to focus on getting through the mine to the alcove where the prisoners were being held.

After what felt like an hour of walking down the main shaft, Garrun motioned for them to follow him down a tunnel to what he told them was the biggest alcove of subfluore they'd found to date. The tunnel here was the smallest they'd encountered yet. They had to hunch to get through, and their shoulders brushed the wooden support beams that kept the tunnel from collapsing.

Finally, they rounded a corner and saw a soft yellow light at the end of the tunnel. Rushing ahead, they found themselves on the upper level of a massive cavern. Here the subfluore crystals weren't confined to metal brackets on the walls, but were jutting out from the stone, creating bright yellow light all around them.

Looking up, Lena could also see some natural light coming in at an angle, an air shaft to help make sure the mines had sufficient fresh air for hard work.

A wooden guardrail was fixed to the rock ledge they were standing on to prevent workers from falling to their deaths forty feet below. They all sneaked up to the rail and peered down. Reeve had to stifle a gasp to not give away their position.

"That's the big brute that was holding the Tahlari in the pool and drowning them," he whispered. Lena could detect a hint of fear in his voice.

They didn't need any explanation of which man Reeve was referring to. Below were rows of dwarves in dirty brown leather garb. They were picking up subfluore crystals from piles along the wall and loading them into mine carts that were on wooden tracks that led off down another tunnel. There were at least ten Tahlari down there with switches. Every time a dwarf would stop for even a moment, they would come down on them with a switch, and the snap would cause a sting of pain, causing a yelp would echo through the cavern. Among these Tahlari stood five cult members adorned in their snake masks, but only one was the size of a fully grown ox standing on its hind legs.

"I thought you said they just needed enough subfluore to hire mercenaries against the Kroll family?" Lena whispered to Garrun.

The dwarf shook his head as his fist tightened on the wooden rail in anger at the sight below. "That crystal is worth a lot of money," he replied. "Waging a war isn't cheap, young elf. I imagine our enemy has its sights on a bit more than just the Krollian throne. It's a multiple win, because by taking the mine, they also cut the Krollians off from their funding in the same move."

Reeve glared at Garrun. "We're not going to let them get that far. My family will not give up what we've earned. Too much is at stake."

"Well, Young Master, the first step is taking down that bull of a man. How do you propose we do that?"

Reeve brought his hand up to his face for a moment, lightly stroking his goatee to think. "Lena, do you have any magic that can strike him down from this distance?" he whispered, turning to her.

Lena felt her face go white as the blood left it. Everyone in the group was now staring at her expectantly. What was she going to do? She knew she'd be on the spot to use her magic at some point, but at such a distance, and with an audience watching?

She looked to Reeve, who was nodding in support, staring deep into her eyes. Something about his look calmed her, but not enough to use advanced magic at this distance.

"Magic will draw too much attention," she lied. "I can use my bow to drop the big one and maybe another two before they notice where it's coming from." She set the two swords down quietly since she didn't have a sheath and pulled out her bow.

"How do I get down there?" Reeve asked Garrun as Lena readied her shot. "We need to be ready to ambush the rest of them once we're found out."

Garrun pointed to a narrow tunnel off to their right. "That spirals down to the lower level. Lena, give us a thirty count before you fire. We'll move in when you're spotted."

Everyone followed Reeve to the tunnel except for Lena, who nocked her arrow and took aim. As she counted to thirty, she watched as the brute took his switch to a younger-looking dwarf who was leaning against the wall for a brief breather from the punishing work. The switch flicked across the dwarf's cheek, creating a gash and spilling blood.

Counting disappeared from Lena's mind as she watched in horror as the switch came down now on the same dwarf's back, ripping his clothes and cutting through to the meat. Everyone below, cult, Tahlari, and dwarf alike all turned to watch the brutal scene.

The victim collapsed to the ground, lying flat on his back, motionless as a puddle of blood grew around him. Lena, still frozen in horror, had no idea what the count was, and drew up higher to aim her shot true. Noticing the sudden movement, the dwarf on the ground reached his arm out and shouted, "Help me!"

The brute turned to see who he was yelling at and spotted Lena standing by the rail on the next level up. With a roar, he brought his fist up above his head, using the entire weight of his hulking body to bring it down on the dwarf's face. A spout of blood came from the dwarf's nose, and he lay completely still.

In absolute panic, Lena loosed the arrow from her bow. Her aim for the brute's neck was true, but having done his evil deed, he turned back towards Lena just as the arrow reached him. It clanged loudly against the mask where the snake's tail hung down past his chin. The shock of the shot sent him staggering back against the wall, but he recovered quickly and roared up at Lena, pointing her out to the others.

The snake-faced cult members stayed with the dwarves while the possessed Tahlari all started running for the tunnel entrance where the rest of her party was waiting. Knowing they'd been found out, Reeve and the other five dwarves came barreling out of the tunnel to confront the assault.

In the confusion, Lena loosed another arrow at the brute. Distracted, he had no time to dodge, but Lena missed his neck. The arrow sank into his shoulder instead. He paused and glanced down towards the arrow, as if mildly agitated, and pulled the arrow from his shoulder. Blood dripped profusely from the wound, but the brute looked mostly unfazed.

Arrow still clenched in his fist, he brought the point hard into the nearest dwarf. The dwarf didn't even have enough time to register a scream, and collapsed to the ground next to his fallen brother.

"Dammit!" screamed Lena. Her every move was making the situation worse. She quickly slung her bow over her shoulder and picked up her swords from the ground, dashing to the tunnel off to the right to help the others.

By the time she made it through the spiraling tunnel to the lower level, the Dark Humans were all on the ground dead, along with another scout dwarf from their party. Seeing Lena had now joined the fight on his level, the brute picked the nearest dwarf up and slung him hard, knocking down two scout dwarves as he grunted and ordered the five cult members to follow him to attack Lena and the others.

Only Lena, Reeve, Garrun, and Dareth were still on their feet as the new wave of enemies reached them. Each armed with a switch and a short sword, the cult came at them hard, screaming an intense war chant behind their snake masks.

Pulling both her swords up to block one of the Tahlari, Lena watched in awe as her assailant chanted a quick spell and the tip of his switch erupted in purple flame. Pushing hard on his sword to push Lena's blades out of the way, he brought the switch crashing into Lena's hand.

She screamed in agony as the fire burnt her hand and caused her to drop one of her swords to the stone floor with a clatter. Seeing she was in trouble, Reeve pulled his sword from the chest of the man he was fighting, and wheeled around to run her assailant through. The man dropped quickly, but before Reeve could recover from his swing, the brute was upon him, bringing his switch down hard on Reeve. A gash opened on his head, and he lost his balance and crumpled to the ground.

Lena stepped in with her remaining sword and drove it hard into the brute's foot. He didn't scream in pain at first because of the shock. Instead, he turned his pain into rage and grabbed two cult members and hurled them in their direction. One of them knocked Lena down, and she quickly flipped to regain her feet.

As she stood, she glimpsed the brute as he made his way down another tunnel and out of sight. Next to her, the two fallen scout dwarves were back on their feet, and together the four dwarves made quick work of the remaining cult members.

Quickly stooping to the fallen Reeve, Lena helped him to his feet. His hair was matted with blood, but otherwise he looked fine. He staggered a bit as he gained his feet, holding his head to feel his cut and steady himself.

Before Lena could speak to him to see if he was okay, she felt a hard jab in her side as Garrun jabbed a finger into her hip. She stepped back, taken aback by the abrupt gesture.

"Did you forget how to count?" he roared at her. She gripped her sword tighter, and then loosened the grip as her instinctual reaction died down.

"I'm sorry, Garrun. I panicked and lost count..."

"You hesitated!" he snapped back, taking a step towards her. Reeve stepped between him and Lena, but Lena used her free hand to guide Reeve out of the way.

"He has a right to be mad," Lena told Reeve. "I didn't stick to the plan. The brute's violence threw me off, and before I knew it, my presence was known. It was all my fault, and I take full responsibility for the delay."

Garrun shrugged. "Not sure how that brings back those two dwarves that brute murdered. Their lives are gone because of you."

Though he was no longer between them, Reeve still cut in, "That's not fair, Garrun. Lena doesn't need that on her conscience right now. We need to focus on the next steps. That means tracking down the brute and finding Karkathi so we can end all of this."

The dwarf master wrinkled his lips at them, as if regretting what he was about to say. "I'm a dwarf of my word. You can take Dareth with you. He can show you where their camp is. Be careful and help him free the dwarves they've taken captive there." Now he turned to look Lena directly in the eyes. "And don't hesitate next time. Maybe you can save more lives."

Lena felt pressure behind her eyes. Though she wasn't one to cry very often, she could feel the tears welling up. If she had known the proper spell, she might have been able to take the brute out more cleanly. If she hadn't hesitated, at least one dwarf the brute had murdered might still be alive. She felt their deaths weighing heavily on her conscience as Reeve spoke.

"Lena, Dareth, we need to move. The brute was limping. We should be able to catch up and take him out. With him out of the picture, our chances of success rise greatly."

They both nodded, and Reeve and Dareth made off for the tunnel that the brute had run down. Lena took one last look at Garrun, who looked as though her presence there was about to make him sick. Dwarves really were stubborn creatures.

Trying to ignore him, she quickly stooped down to take a belt and two sheaths from the dead cult members. She could feel Garrun looking at her the whole time she did this. Once she had her new swords settled in their sheaths on her hips, she gave him a slight, awkward nod, and took off after the other two, ready to face the brute again and end his reign of terror.

Chapter Twelve

IN THE SHADOWS

The tunnels through the mountain were all straight, but there were so many veering off in all directions, it was impossible to tell which one the brute had stumbled off down. Lena tried to check for a blood trail, but the trail stopped as if the brute had tied up his foot during his staggering through the tunnels. Within the hour they found themselves all the way through one of the exit shafts with no sign of him anywhere.

Night had set in on the forest, the darkness pressing in on them as they exited the mountain. Disappointed that they weren't able to finish off their giant foe, the trio set their stuff down for a brief rest. Lena felt a pang of guilt as she looked at Dareth and saw a single tear running down his face.

Unsure of whether she should say anything, she decided it was probably better to engage. "I'm so sorry for your loss."

Dareth was quiet for a moment, and Lena was expecting him to lash out at her like Garrun had, but what she got back was a much gentler tone. "Aye. Lost several good dwarves down there. Wasn't any of it your fault, though. Garrun is built tough. Has to be to manage all the hard-headed dwarves that work the mines."

Reeve walked up to Dareth and placed a hand on his shoulder. "Was Garrun the one who allowed my family to take charge of Mt. Fluore?" he asked.

"Aye. He was never much for ruling. Didn't want the dwarves involved in politics, only profit. When your grandfather showed up with his family and a whole tribe of freed Tahlari, Garrun knew he had to step down. It was part of the reward for taking out Vairtross and ridding the land of the plague that they were. I feel like part of his anger now centers on that decision and whether he would have handled this whole ordeal with the cult better than old Elric."

Lena still wasn't sure what to make of the dwarves. So far, they had been very gruff and somewhat rude. Where the Kroll family had accepted her as a substitute for her father, the dwarves seemed to see right through her, knowing things would go better if Umbra had indeed come instead of her.

Pulling her cloak down over her eyes, Lena didn't want to look at Dareth. Though he was being kind, it still felt like he was secretly judging her. "Do we stay and wait for the brute to come out, or do we move on to the camp?" she asked, working hard to busy herself with her pack and avoid eye contact with Dareth.

"Too many tunnels he could have gone down. A few of them were emergency exit shafts that came out on different faces of the mountain. I think we're best suited to go to the camp to free the captured dwarves."

Reeve nodded. "I agree. If we can take out Karkathi and his sorcerer, I don't think the brute will have anything left to fight for."

Seeing the devastation the brute was capable of, Lena knew she would rather wait and take him out now while he was injured and weak, but as the other two wanted to go to the camp, she was outvoted on their next move.

They packed their things and headed off through the forest. After a few steps, Lena felt a tingling on the back of her head, as if someone was watching them. She turned quickly back towards the mountain, but saw nothing but rock, trees, and darkness. She made a mental note to watch their backs as they traveled and sped off after Reeve and Dareth.

The dwarf had assured them that the camp wasn't far. It had been a quick twenty-minute run through the woods after he and the other scouts had been spotted earlier, so a brisk walk would easily get them there in under an hour.

If the estimate were true, the hour went by quickly as they anxiously made their way through the dark woods. Lena's frequent checks behind them showed they weren't being followed, but she was still anxious about what lay ahead. The darkness gave them some much-needed cover until a few minutes later when the cult's camp came into sight.

It was much rougher than the permanently placed Tahlari village she'd been to the previous night. Animal hides were stretched out over rough wooden poles to make tents. There was no central area for people to meet, just tents spread apart far enough that fires could be lit without sending anything up in smoke.

They could see cult members huddled around the fires, cooking and talking with each other. In the dim light, she could see that many of them had removed their masks, better to eat and talk without.

From their cover behind two particularly wide pine trees, Dareth pointed out the longer tent on the opposite side of the camp. "That belongs to the leader and his sorcerer. The dwarves are likely around there. I say if we play this right, we can free them and use the extra bodies to overpower Karkathi."

Lena looked at Reeve to see what he thought of this plan to free the dwarves before killing the leader. It made sense to her, but she could see his lip twitching in anger. "We need to take out Karkathi before he's onto us. He may not be the sorcerer, but he has magic from the pool too."

She hated to admit it, but she had to agree with Dareth. "He's powerful," Lena told Reeve. "It makes the most sense to free the prisoners first. Don't worry..." she added, "...Karkathi will get what's coming to him in the end. He won't hurt any more Tahlari, or your family."

The words came before she realized she couldn't be certain she could keep that promise, but she still had to stick with the plan that made the most sense tactically, and not the one fueled by anger because of her inappropriate feelings for Reeve.

"Fine," he said, almost pouting. "I trust your judgement, Lena, and Dareth's scouting skills as well."

"Good," said Dareth. "Let's follow the treeline around the camp so we can get closer to the big tent without being seen."

Off to the south, just out of sight, Karkathi watched as the dwarf, the elf, and the human started moving along the trees to the other side of his camp. He recognized the human as the man who had interrupted his last Virmorph ceremony and lived to tell the tale. Reeve Kroll.

He bared his teeth, and his nostrils flared at the man and his companions. While he didn't quite have the powers of Malak, something in the Virmorph pool had given him slight magical abilities. A tingling sensation running through him whispered a truth in his head: he and Reeve couldn't both survive this night.

Focusing his attention on the dwarf in Reeve's accompaniment didn't send him any signals. Likely just a scout they had chased away earlier. But this elf in the lavender robe? She glowed slightly white in the darkness. For a moment, Karkathi had to question whether or not she was actually glowing, but given the fact they were trying to sneak, it seemed that she was only glowing white in his sight.

What could that mean? Magic of The Light? Magic for the weak. As they passed by him and out of sight behind a cropping of trees, he noticed she had a bow strung across her back. A magic weapon? It didn't seem so. The weapon didn't have the same glow as the rest of her body did. Why carry such a mundane weapon if you could wield magic?

The bigger question was, why was she here? Karkathi knew of the great Umbra of Zelira who had obliterated the kingdom of Vairtross and most of its inhabitants. He had been a young boy when it had happened, but he had heard tales of the feat from Malak, who used to be a High Shaman there.

A branch cracked behind him, interrupting his train of thought. He didn't even bother to turn and look, as he sensed no danger there. A moment later, two big, beefy hands landed on the tree he was peering around, and Karkathi turned to see his enforcer beside him, propping himself up for support.

"Bok, you appear to have injured your foot," he said with a chill in his voice. "I assume you sustained this injury as you were failing me?"

He couldn't see the expression on Bok's face because of the snake mask he was still wearing, but he imagined the brute was grimacing based on the pain in his voice.

"Was stabbed," the brute grunted at him. "An elf witch and her companions attacked. I'm the only one left."

"So we only have the one cart of subfluore we extracted yesterday?"

Bok hung his head a bit. "'fraid so."

Karkathi gritted his teeth. "That's enough to sell for a few mercenaries, Bok, but how are we supposed to fund an empire if we don't have a surplus? We can't even take Mt. Fluore without raising a massive army, let alone reclaim my father's kingdom in Darmark."

"Apologies, My Lord," said Bok, subdued like a child being chastised by a parent.

"You're lucky you're such a good enforcer, Bok, or I wouldn't care to waste my energy healing your foot." Karkathi looked down at the brute's bare foot and saw a blood-soaked piece of cloth there. He removed the wrap and saw the slit where a sword had impaled it.

"The elf witch did this to you?" Karkathi asked as he examined the wound. Bok nodded. "Right," said Karkathi, pulling up his hand to the wound. Purple light formed between his fingers. "We must be careful around her then and also make sure she meets a terrible fate very soon. Don't yell," he added as he pushed the purple energy into the brute's wound.

Bok grunted and strained, but he kept his voice down as Karkathi burned the wound, stopping the flow of blood. He examined the healed wound by the purple light of his hand. The foot looked like a piece of cooked meat that had been sitting on the fire too long, but the bleeding had stopped.

Putting his foot gently down on the ground, Bok tested his weight on it. "Go see Malak for some henbane to take the pain away. Tell Rizak to take the dwarves to the dungeons. We'll conduct our ritual there, and if that fails, we'll kill them and bring them back to life so they can obey us like the others."

Bok nodded and began to hobble away, when Karkathi called after him. "Oh, and Bok. Before Malak burns you some henbane, tell him to send the dogs after those three."

CHAPTER THIRTEEN

THE DOGS OF BALADAN

A cage was set at the back of the camp near the woods. Inside the cage, they could see the five dwarves who had been taken during the raid at the mines. The dwarves were sprawled out on the bottom of the cage, their clothes ripped, beards and faces matted with blood and dirt.

Lena had to place a hand on Dareth's shoulder to keep him from running up to the cage. He turned and gave her a dirty look.

"No one is around; we need to go get them!" Dwarves really had no patience. She supposed that would happen when you only had hundreds of years to live instead of thousands. Glancing at Reeve, she wondered why he wasn't much more impatient than either of them.

Just as he said this, they saw movement past the cage. It was coming from a dilapidated stone arch next to a broken-down wall. They saw the head at first, near to the ground, but as the head got bigger, the body appeared underneath. The figure was a cult member wearing a snake mask, coming up from a set of stairs that led down into the ground.

Dareth nodded at Lena, thanking her for holding him back. Lena slowly shook her head. Her first encounter with dwarves hadn't been a great experience so far. They had all been blunt in their speech and quick to act without thinking. Although, given the circumstances, she could see that she wasn't catching them at their best.

"I think if you drop that one with an arrow, we should be free to help them make a quick escape. I don't see any other sentries coming."

Lena's heart skipped as Reeve spoke to her through the darkness. She moved closer to him, pushing her shoulder against his, pretending she needed to get closer to communicate more quietly.

"It's dim lighting, but I can make a clean shot," she said, pulling her bow off her back and nocking an arrow. She had never gone hunting at night, as many nocturnal creatures back in Zelira and the academy were predatory and not much good for eating or making clothes.

Despite the bad lighting, she felt her thumb knuckle reach its anchor point at the bottom of her right ear, exhaled to steady herself, and aimed the arrowhead for the man's neck. She tried to ignore that she could feel Reeve's eyes on her as she aligned her shot.

A gurgle sounded as the arrow found its mark, but it wasn't loud enough to alert anyone nearby except the imprisoned dwarves. They all stared as the sentry fell to the ground with a dull thud and then traced the arrow's path back to where the shot had come from.

Dareth made to step out of the trees and run to his comrades, but froze when a beast came out from the nearest tent and raced on its four legs to smell the body. The beast had the build and size of a large dog, but this dog appeared to have walked straight out of Baladan's plane. Its muzzle was narrower than the large fluffy yellow dogs Lena was used to seeing back home. The mouth of the beast hung open, the opening originating back further under its tall wispy ears, allowing the mouth to unhinge unnaturally wide. The dog's body was muscular, and the fur shot up in red, semi-luminescent spikes.

As it pulled its head up from smelling the body, it fixed its dimly glowing red eyes toward the trio hiding in the trees. A low growl erupted from deep within the hound as it began slowly stalking towards them.

Lena quickly drew another arrow and fired it at the dog. It hit it in the shoulder, but the dog didn't even wince. It just kept walking towards them, its growl growing deeper, its needle-like teeth poised to bite. Lena gasped as more sets of glowing eyes appeared in the darkness behind the beast.

"Run!" she whispered to Reeve and Dareth. Neither of the males moved, frozen with fright at the sight of the dogs closing in. "Now!" she said, grabbing them by their clothes and pulling them out of their trance.

They quickly snapped to and stumbled a few steps before they gained their footing and took off running back into the woods. Lena hung back behind them, ready to turn and fight to give the other two a chance to escape.

Feeling back for her quiver, she could feel that she only had five arrows left. Given that they hadn't even confronted Karkathi or his sorcerer yet, it seemed a very sad few too many arrows to get the job done.

Glancing back, she could see the dog was still hot on their trail. It was now joined by at least six other dogs. They had fanned out into a wide line, the dogs on the end moving faster, and it looked like they were trying to flank them and cut off their escape.

Trees were whipping past as she sped through the woods, looking for any place that would give them a tactical advantage against the dogs. Could they swim? Could they climb trees?

She'd never been up against any beast the likes of what was chasing them, so she couldn't be sure.

Grabbing an arrow to nock it as they ran, she quickly planted her foot and spun to take quick aim at the leader. She could see her first arrow sticking out of his shoulder, but this time her aim was truer. The arrowhead found the space between the dog's eyes, dropping it to the ground.

She stared in horror as the dog dropped to the ground, erupting in a purple light so bright she had to look away for a second. When she looked back, she saw that where the dog had fallen, a Tahlari tribe member was now sprawled out on the ground, an arrow sticking up from his head.

A pit grew instantly in her stomach, and she felt like she might vomit. Instead, she found her legs and turned to sprint off away from the other dogs that were closing in.

What kind of sick and twisted magic was this? Humans had been turned into these feral dogs. To what end? It was clear that Karkathi was trying to amass a terrible army, not only of cult members and Tahlari men but also of dark and twisted creatures.

She could hear the skittering of the dogs' feet across the forest floor growing louder. The crunch of twigs and dead pine needles grew to a roar in her ear, and she could see dogs running out the corner of her eyes, feeling the air they were kicking up like wind blowing her cloak. They were closing in.

Up ahead, she saw Reeve look back and notice she was in trouble. She felt a tug at the back of her cloak, and her heart sank as she realized a hound had a hold of her. Reeve was too far away to help, and she knew if she fell over she was done for.

In one swift movement, her right hand grabbed the sword from her left hip, and she swung around with the blade in a big arc, unsheathing and striking in one swift movement. The dog barely yelped before its head was cleaved from its body.

Down in a crouch, her left hand found the right blade and, without even looking toward the attack, she struck out at the next dog that was launching through the air at her. The blade caught its underbelly, spilling its insides out on the ground beside her.

She could see dark shadows flitting between the trees, and knew many more dogs were coming for them. Suddenly, she felt a hand on her shoulder and jumped. Reeve was standing there, deep concern and awe on his face. Giving him a quick nod, she took his hand to help get to her feet. She didn't dare to look at the aftermath of her attack as the two dogs glowed purple. She felt she would lose what was left of her mental stability if she saw what she had just done to the poor possessed Tahlari.

Taking off at a run again, Lena searched deep in her mind for some sort of spell. Something, anything, that would help them fend off so many wild dogs. The only things she could think of were shield and healing spells. Nothing that would keep the dogs away indefinitely, especially since her magical stamina was so weak. No shield would hold for long.

After several more yards of running, Lena could see that the trees broke into a small clearing up ahead. Unsure if this would provide any tactical advantage, the trio barreled forward until they came upon a shrine set within a rocky area. The edges of the rock ground it sat on curled upwards to form a large basin across the ground.

Carved of rock, and smooth as marble, the statue depicted the god Solana in all his glory. He was coming down from the top of the statue, arms spread wide, his robes flowing down to surround a small bowl midway down the shrine. A vine with white flowers grew along the base of the statue.

It was a beautiful sight to behold, but Lena didn't have time to decipher the purpose of the shrine as she heard the rapid patter of feet behind her again. She stumbled over the lip of the large rock basin, and this slowed her just enough that a dog slammed her hard into the ground.

Her swords fell out of her hands and clattered across the empty basin. She threw her arms up to block the gnashing jaws of the dog from ripping her throat out. Over the angry growls of the dog, she could hear Dareth and Reeve fighting to combat their own attackers, and the situation felt hopeless as more and more dogs joined the fray.

Lena was screaming as the dog's head came down at her time after time, and she knew she wouldn't be able to block the attacks forever. Somewhere above her, she heard dogs whining, and prayed to Solana that meant that the other two were winning their fights and could somehow break free to run away and save themselves.

Thinking of a shock spell she'd learned in her third year at the academy, Lena began speaking in tongues between her grunts of effort to keep the dog at bay. Yellow light formed in her hand, gaining brightness and heat. The dog backed off a little, wary of the new light in the darkness. Instead, it lashed out with its claws, slashing her midsection.

She screamed in pain before she could finish the spell, and the light faded. Another dog had rushed her and sunk its teeth deep into her arm. The needle-like teeth created not only a deep puncture, but a burning sensation, and she pulled her arms in tight to keep them from being bitten again.

This reflex was a mistake as her first attacker saw an opening and lunged its head in, jaws aiming right for her throat. Her eyes grew wide as she realized this was the end.

A deep scream echoed through the air, pulling her from the vision. Up above her, she saw a small, muscular arm thrust through the air just above her face, the glint of a dagger flashing as it entered the dog's mouth and was driven upward into the beast's brain.

Lena heard Dareth grunt in pain as the fatal blow caused the dog's sharp teeth to sink into his arm. With a yell, the dwarf pulled his dagger back out, red blood gushing down onto Lena's chest as the wound opened up. The dog fell down hard onto her. She felt crushed, but happy to be alive.

As Dareth pulled his arm back, his own blood soaking his sleeve, another dog lunged in and took the dwarf's arm into its mouth, shaking him back and forth trying to break the bones and tear his flesh.

Unable to move under the weight of the dog, Lena stared wide-eyed and helpless as Dareth stabbed at the dog's head with his other dagger. The dog slowed, but still kept shaking the dwarf until Reeve popped up from the darkness and ran his sword through the beast.

Purple light lit the darkness as the dead dog turned back into a Tahlari, and Dareth stumbled backwards screaming in pain, cradling his mangled arm. Reeve moved quickly, kicking the dog off of Lena and pulling her up forcefully from the ground. He quickly pushed her and Dareth towards the shrine, struck another dog down, and jumped into the basin to stand by the shrine as well.

They all gawked as a yellow light shone up from the ground in a small circle around them. The dogs that were left tried pushing against the circle, but they couldn't seem to get through. Their frustration and anger were clear as they paced around the circle, slobber dripping down their hungry jowls in anticipation of one of them moving away from the statue.

"Gah!" Dareth howled in pain, still cradling his arm. "What is this?"

Lena examined the light circle and glanced back at the statue to see Solana's hands on the shrine were glowing in the darkness. "It's a shrine of Solana," said Lena. "It must be offering us protection." She looked down into the bowl of the statue and saw water sitting at the bottom. "Not sure if this water will be of any use to us?" she asked, not sure that the other two would have any type of answer for her.

"It's just water," Reeve chimed in, waving his sword at each dog as it passed just in case the barrier broke and he needed to strike. "The Tahlari use this shrine to multiply what little water they have during drought. It has saved them countless times over the decades."

Lena raised her eyebrows at Reeve, not sure how he could possibly know something like that. Before she could voice this thought, however, a deep, soothing voice spoke from behind her.

"Zoon aloon, ateum rapata."

She turned to face the statue, placing her hands on the edge of the bowl and staring into the smiling face of Solana.

"I told you, it's just water," said Reeve. "It's no help."

"Did you hear that?" Lena shot at him.

He shook his head no. "All I hear are the dogs."

The voice had been loud and commanding. There was no way he couldn't have heard it. Unless...

She turned towards the dogs, throwing her hands wide as the statue's pose behind her.

"Zoon aloon, atem rapta," she said forcefully. Nothing happened.

"Lena, what are you doing? Do you know a spell to kill them?" asked Reeve excitedly.

Ignoring him, Lena held her hands higher and screamed at the top of her voice. "Zoon aloon, ateum rapata!"

A circle of yellow light pushed out from her body and shot out into the darkness. It passed through the dogs, who yelped like scared puppies, and on past them out into the dark forest until it dissipated.

Looking down at the surrounding ground, the trio stared in awe as the dogs were no more. Tahlari men lie around them, grunting and rubbing their heads, looking up to the three of them standing next to the statue.

Whatever spell Solana had just given her, it had not only saved their lives, but had broken the spell on the Tahlari men as well. Lena briefly smiled.

Chapter Fourteen

KAEL

H is arm was mangled and broken beyond use. Dareth grunted in pain as he slouched against the shrine, trying to compose himself enough to discuss their plans to move on and help the other dwarves still trapped in the cage.

"Don't worry about them just yet," Reeve said, placing a hand on the dwarf's good shoulder to comfort him.

"Don't worry? Argh! How can I not worry? The bloody dogs are a good indicator that they know we're here!"

"He's right," said Lena. "We can't stay long. The dwarves are in danger, and Karkathi may have fled already."

"He hasn't," said a voice from behind them. Lena and Reeve turned away from Dareth to see who had spoken. One of the Tahlari men who had just transformed back from being a dog was trying to gain his feet. They could see two long wounds running along his back as if he had been whipped at some point recently.

The man stood and moved awkwardly over to them as if he didn't quite remember how to walk on two feet again. They watched him guardedly, not sure if he was still violent. It was obvious he could read this on their faces as he waved his hands at them.

"Don't worry. I can see that the trees are green again."

Their looks of guardedness turned quickly to confusion. "Everything was so gray in there... when I was under their control. Not sure what you did, elf, but you seem to have broken their control."

"You said that Karkathi won't have fled?" Reeve cut in. "How do you know that?"

The Tahlari man shrugged. "As we were being led to Malak to be turned into dogs, others were being ordered to take the hostages to the dungeons. Karkathi said something about sacrificing them in a ritual."

"Then we have to get moving!" Dareth roared as he tried to stand, but his arm was causing him too much pain to move. His howl of pain echoed through the dark, silent night.

Reeve turned to Lena. "Can you use your magic to heal him?"

"It might be beyond repair," said Lena, avoiding Reeve's gaze. The truth was she'd seen some amazing healing in her time, but the last time she'd tried to heal someone it drained her energy so much she couldn't leave her dormitorium for the rest of the day. Healing with The Light required transferring your own energy to another, and if you were weak in magic, it took extra life force to get the job done.

"Please," said Reeve, placing a hand on hers. His touch felt warm, and she turned to look into his eyes. His eyes were deep, troubled, and desperate for a solution to help their guide. He had rushed in to save her from the dogs, after all. It was the least she could do to try.

"Okay," she said, pulling her hand sharply away before she let her mind wander to other ideas. Cracking her knuckles and wiggling her fingers, she tried to summon her memory of healing spells. As she remembered, words formed on her lips. When she spoke the words, her hands began glowing yellow, not a ball of energy this time, but a radiance straight from her palms.

As she touched her hands to Dareth's mangled arm, she could feel energy moving from her core and out through her hands. Dareth whimpered as his arm glowed. It was so bright that Lena couldn't see what was going on with the arm, but could sense that it was repairing and restoring its normal form.

After a minute, the light on his arm faded, and Lena knew that the restoration was almost done. She slowed her speech and tapered off the volume of her words until the words faded to nothing.

Looking down at Dareth's arm, she could see it was back to its normal appearance. He was wiggling his fingers and testing them out.

"How does it feel?" she asked him.

"A bit sore, but nothing worse than working a day in the mines," he said, using the water bowl on the statue above his head to pull himself to his feet.

Lena tested her own fingers, moving her arms a bit, trying to feel her own strength. It was odd, but she didn't feel drained of energy at all. She looked up at the statue of Solana on the shrine, its face looking knowingly back at her. Between the successful healing and the transformation of the dogs back to Tahlari, she knew the magic of the statue had something to do with it.

"That was amazing," said Reeve as he threw an arm around Dareth to help steady him. "Lena, it truly is a blessing to have you here on this mission."

Lena felt her face flush red again. So far she'd bungled most of the mission, and she owed the rest to Dareth saving her life and the smiling statue before her. The silence hung in the moment, and when Lena didn't answer, Reeve just smiled and turned back to the Tahlari man.

"What was your name, sir?" Reeve asked him.

"Treyvon," replied the young man.

"Treyvon," Reeve stated. "Don't think I don't remember you killing my cousins."

The Tahlari looked shocked and opened his mouth the explain, but Reeve held up his hand to stop him. "I understand you were under their spell, and whatever you did to fight the madness saved my life as you struggled not to kill me. So I guess I should be thanking you."

"No," said Treyvon. "What I did is inexcusable. It still haunts me. I'm so..."

Reeve held up his hand again. "Apologies later. We need to move. You said there were dungeons that the dwarves were being taken to. Where could there possibly be dungeons around here?"

"There's a broken arch by where the dwarves were being held," he said. "That's a stairway that leads to the dungeons and sanctums underground."

"I'm still confused," Lena said. "Dungeons in the middle of the forest?" And then it hit her. "Unless..."

Treyvon nodded. "The old dungeons of Vairtross were never destroyed. Just the kingdom above. Umbra the Great did a good job obliterating the kingdom, but it seems like he missed a few pieces. Was probably too busy building that shrine for the Tahlari," he said, pointing past Lena. "I can't complain though. The water that it multiplies has saved us from drought many times over the years."

Umbra the Great? Lena turned slowly and looked again at the statue of Solana. The right side of her top lip curled up in bewilderment. This time it looked like the god's smile was more mocking than caring. What was her father's fixation with statues, anyway?

Not knowing that Lena was processing all of this, Reeve continued on with business. "Treyvon, can you lead us to the dungeons?"

The young Tahlari nodded. He pointed at the other young Tahlari men who had transformed from the dogs, now gaining their feet and gathering around them.

"They can go back to their villages. I will come with you and help. I owe you that much."

The cage was empty when they got back to the camp. Sentries were still walking around at regular intervals, but there were noticeably fewer people around. Lena had a sinking feeling that Treyvon was right. Going down into the dungeons felt like volunteering to jump into a pit of snakes. Given the masks of the cult members, this feeling was almost literal.

They waited silently in the trees, timing the laps and noting the routes of the sentries. Finally, when they could time a break where the broken archway was clear, they stole away across the opening by the cage, and down into the stairwell past the broken arch.

The wooden stairs were thin planks that barely held the length of their feet as they climbed down, and were steep, almost like a ladder. Lena guessed her father had destroyed the stairs and called it good. Someone else had come in more recently and built this makeshift set that she now prayed to Solana would hold them.

It was nearly pitch black at the bottom of the stairs, with just a pinprick of light up ahead. "Are you able to cast a light with your magic?" Reeve called up to her as he entered the darkness.

Lena shut her eyes hard, thankful for the darkness covering up her disgrace and embarrassment. "I can give it a go," she said. Even as the light came easily to her hand and gave them a dim glow to move forward with, she could feel her energy drain from this simple magic task. She began a jog that almost bordered on a run. She hoped it was taken as haste to reach the captured dwarves, and not the need to get into the light so she could kill the spell and stop using magic.

With her light, she could see they were now in a long hallway of very dark-gray stone. The walls were covered in a white film, most likely some kind of fungus that found refuge in the dark, damp environment.

When they reached the light at the end of the hall, they were greeted with a long, rectangular room bathed in torchlight. It looked like they were on the middle of three floors, and all along the perimeter of the room were cells of prisoners. Ramps sat at each end of the room, leading up and down to the next level. The bottom level had another large archway at the opposite end, presumably leading to the sanctums Treyvon had mentioned.

"My people were kidnapped and brought here. At least until they could take us to that purple pool to drown us. Your dwarf friends will be here as well."

Lena leaned over the wooden railing and looked down. She could see all the downtrodden Tahlari slumped in their cells. Looking around the level they were on, she got a better view of the conditions they were forced to live in.

There were five men per cell, and no beds. All the men were covered in dirt and blood, slouched over and weak. Some cells had a deflated waterskin hung from the bars, the prisoners desperate to have them refilled.

Something caught Lena's eye as she was looking around. Feet appeared slowly from the ramp one level down. As a reflex, she immediately pulled her bow and nocked an arrow, crouching low behind the wooden rail. Her companions, following her lead, also crouched down.

"What is it?" asked Dareth.

"Guard," she whispered, setting her sights on the man's head that had now come into view. The man wore the same metal snake mask as the others and had a sword holstered at his side. As she aimed her shot, she also noticed a string across his chest, indicating that this one carried a bow. As he moved his head, she now saw the quiver on his back full of arrows.

A quick glance around the room showed her that this was the only guard around. Her sight zeroed in on the man's chest, then to the right a bit so it would hit him just left of center. Judging from his slow walking pace, she moved back left a little and let the arrow fly.

A gasp and a clamoring could be heard below as the prisoners below watched, shocked, as the guard outside their cell crumbled silently to the ground in a heap.

Lena pointed to the nearest ramp, and they all followed her down to the lower level, where the guard had just fallen. Lena, Reeve, and Dareth ignored the immediate pleas of the prisoners as they ran past, looking instead to see if the guard had keys. They lost Treyvon along the way as he stopped to talk to the desperate Tahlari, grasping their hands through the bars and whispering to them in comfort.

Reaching the body, Reeve immediately found the metal ring that held the cell keys. Snatching them, he ran back to Treyvon, and the two of them began freeing the prisoners from their cells.

Lena stayed with the fallen guard, examining the bow on his back. It was much more refined than the one she had scrapped together in the woods before being abducted by the Tahlari. This one was made of sanded yew, a much higher-quality finish. The arrow rest and the tips were inlaid with a bone plating to help make the connection of the string to the bow more sturdy.

She asked Dareth to lift the body so she could get the bow off the dead man. As he did so, she stared in awe as she stood with it, grasping the bone rest in her left hand, and the string in her right. The string itself was another marvel, as it appeared to be spun of fine silk. She had only seen this type of bowstring on the weapons of soldiers, a rarity she was never given access to, being expected to use magic instead.

Even among soldiers, silk strings were rare. Silkworms were only known to be raised on the plateaus above the canyon kingdom of Nimbur. She gave the string a pluck, and the twanging sound reverberated through her soul. This was by far the finest bow she had ever held, and here it had been, strapped to the back of some nameless guard who held it in case he had a prisoner on the run.

Tossing her old bow down onto the body of the guard, Lena strung the magnificent new bow over her back, and Dareth gave her a knowing look, smiling. "Looting bodies now, are we?" he asked her with a smirk.

"It's a nice bow, why wouldn't I?" she asked as she snatched the arrows from his quiver. "Never pass on a chance to upgrade, Master Dwarf," she added with a slight smile.

Dareth didn't answer, only smirked as she quivered the arrows and walked off to join Reeve and Treyvon in freeing prisoners.

They caught up with the others past two empty cells, while they were unlocking the third. "The Tahlari from the last cell said they saw the dwarves being dragged through the main arch over there. We may be too late," said Reeve as they approached.

"No!" said Dareth, a little louder than intended, and he slapped his hand over his mouth in response. Whispering, he added, "I mean, I won't accept it. We still have to go after them."

"Agreed," said Reeve. "They also said Karkathi is with them to perform the ritual. Now is our chance."

Lena nodded. "Treyvon, stay here and free your people. We will go on ahead."

The lock clicked as she said this, and the Tahlari eagerly waiting on the other side rushed out. Treyvon embraced the first one that came out. "Darius! We're free!" he said excitedly as he clapped the other man on the back, crying.

After the young men had all rushed out, an elderly villager meandered his way forward. It was an odd sight since all the prisoners and Dark Humans she had seen so far were young men. The old man's face was battered and bruised, but he smiled at them all as he exited.

"Why are you here among these young men?" Lena asked, wondering if there were other elders in the surrounding cells.

The beaten old man just chuckled. "I had the audacity to fight them off when they tried to take my grandson. They also thought I would have knowledge as a village elder."

"Knowledge of what?" Reeve asked nervously. Lena looked at him and could see he looked really uncomfortable, tugging at the collar of his tunic.

The old man turned to smile at Reeve. "They had a lot of questions about ancient practices of turning men into beasts of the earth," he said, "of which I honestly knew nothing about."

Reeve nodded his head and grabbed Lena's shoulder to lead her away. "We must go if we are to save the dwarves," he said hastily.

Before they took two steps, the man called after them, "Don't worry, Kael ed' Evania. I've told them nothing of you."

CHAPTER FIFTEEN

SACRIFICE

"What did he just call you?" asked Lena as she briskly followed Reeve, who was hastening away from her. She could hear Dareth following behind her, but her attention was mostly on Reeve, who had left the old man as if he had just insulted his mother.

"We have to keep moving," Reeve said, trying to brush her off.

"Don't know about you, but I can talk and walk at the same time," she whispered to him as they passed through the archway.

Reeve huffed and then turned back to face Lena. "He called me Kael ed' Evania," said Reeve. "It means 'Bridge of the People'. My mother was Tahlari. Can we unpack this another time, please?" At that, he turned and continued his brisk walk.

"Guess he can't talk and walk," said Dareth, shrugging and pulling out his daggers, ready for their next confrontation.

Lena blew a strand of hair out of her face and followed them. She wasn't sure what the big deal about Reeve being half-Tahlari was, but it was obviously a big secret among the Kroll family.

They found themselves in another hall, but this one had dim lighting from the torches spaced far apart on the wall. Archways filled the hall on both sides, leading off to different areas of the dungeon.

"How do we know where they went?" Dareth asked exasperatedly. "Guess which of the seven paths they took? It's like walking through the mines! You either already know your way, or you're hopelessly lost!"

Lena looked at all the open doorways, unsure what the right answer was. She cast more light into her hand and, ignoring the feeling of fatigue that set in from using the simple spell, walked down the hallway examining the floor for clues.

"Fate calls," whispered an eerie voice in the air.

Lena turned quickly to Reeve and Dareth. "What?" she asked them, confused.

Reeve looked at her, puzzled. "We didn't say anything," he said.

She cocked her head a bit, and a shiver ran up her spine. Looking at each of the tunnels that went off in different directions, she closed her eyes and listened again.

"You will fail," the voice said.

Whipping around and opening her eyes, she settled her gaze on the doorway in the middle of the hall behind her. She approached slowly, holding her light up to get a better look.

The doorway looked like any other in the hallway, except this one had an etching above the entrance. Pressing closer, she could see the odd symbol, caked in dust, but still distinguishable. It was that of a serpent, curled in a circle and biting its own tail. In the middle of the serpent, diagonally across, sat a writing quill.

The symbol seemed to glow faintly red as she looked at it, but when she blinked, it was just dull stone again. She took a step back as the air from the tunnel hummed, a deep bellowing. She looked at her two companions, but neither seemed to hear it.

"Is that the way?" asked Dareth.

Lena shook her head furiously. "No! Definitely not that way. We shouldn't go down there." Thinking quickly, she pulled her light low and examined the ground. The same layer of dust that had covered the symbol was also on the floor. She quickly identified scuff marks in the dust where the dwarves had been dragged, alongside human footprints. They led off down a tunnel on the left, opposite the tunnel with the sigil.

She breathed a sigh of relief. "The marks in the dust show they went this way," she said, pointing off down the tunnel where the dust was cleared. "Let's move," she added, turning to look at the ominous arch behind her one last time. She could feel the chill of goosebumps run down her arms, and quickly hurried the opposite way down the right corridor.

Through the doorway they found themselves at the top of a sunken chamber. Tiered ledges circled the dimly lit room, descending toward a flat floor at its center. The tiers served both as seating for those who once gathered here and as steps leading down to the lower levels. It reminded Lena of the amphitheater back in Zelira, only this one enveloped the space.

Standing in the sanctum's bowl were at least a dozen cult members, all standing in a circle surrounding the one unmasked man at the center. Reeve recognized him immediately as Karkathi. He tapped Lena and Dareth on their shoulders and whispered, "That's him."

Lena gasped as she recognized his face from her vision from Solana. The tall nose and horrifying gaunt eyes that stared hatred into her soul before he plunged her under the water to drown. Now, he was standing in the middle of the circle of men, his colorful robes billowing out around him, a sharpened staff in his hands.

A lone dwarf lay on a stone slab beneath Karkathi, struggling against his rope constraints and gasping. He was already covered in blood and grime, injured in the struggle, and now the cult had gathered to perform their ritual. No other dwarves were in sight.

It wasn't even Karkathi that made Lena's stomach drop. It was the man standing behind him. A deep laugh echoed through the chamber, and she knew it was him. The brute they had faced in the mines, back to finish the job. Still clad in his mask, she couldn't see his face, but there was no way he could be mistaken for anyone else.

The laugh made the others in the ritual look up as the brute pointed in their direction. Karkathi looked up, a smile curling on his lips. "Was hoping you would join us!" he yelled gleefully at them. "You can join the others!"

He stepped to the side and gestured behind him. The other captured dwarves were laid out in a line, wounds in their chests from the pointed staff Karkathi carried.

"No!" yelled Dareth as he tried to lunge forward, but Reeve grabbed his shirt and held him back.

"You charge down there, you're dead," he snapped at him, pushing him backwards as he released his shirt. "Lena," he added, but she was already in motion.

The arrow was nocked and ready in an instant; her aim set on Karkathi's chest. "Drop the staff!" she yelled down at him. The new bow felt perfect in her grip, the limbs bending just right, the string responding well in her grip. The bone inlay provided the perfect grip to steady her shot.

"You don't scare me, elf. You don't have half the skill of your father."

The line hit her like the sudden shock of a janari. "How do you know who my father is?" she asked, her fingers itching to release the arrow now instead of waiting for the answer.

Karkathi shrugged. "He's the only other elf ever to come around these parts. Plus, you look like him a bit."

That line definitely grated on her nerves. Why couldn't anyone ever say she looked like her mother, who was so beautiful that her father had named his kingdom after her?

When she didn't answer, Karkathi continued talking. "Umbra may have decimated Vairtross, but they are coming back strong, and my vendetta against the Kroll family is even stronger. The three of you are inconsequential. Please," he added to the cult members around him, gesturing for them to kill Lena and her companions.

Without hesitation, Lena loosed her arrow. The shaft flew true, but instead of hitting Karkathi, it sank into the brute's biceps as he stepped in front of his master to block it.

Lena almost dropped her bow in shock. That was twice that her arrows had failed to faze the giant. The brute pulled the arrow from his arm and snapped it. Then, staring up at them, he ripped off his snake mask and crushed the metal between his hands, crumpling it into a ball.

His face was grotesque. It looked like he had been burnt badly at some point in his life, and it hadn't healed properly.

Lena wondered if her father had caused his pain when he had burnt Vairtross to the ground.

She didn't have long to dwell on this as he laughed manically, pushing aside the other cult members and barreling towards the three of them, pulling a broadsword from a scabbard at his hip.

Quickly slinging her bow and her back, she grabbed her two swords and prepared for impact. She glanced quickly from side-to-side and could see that Reeve was ready with his sword, and Dareth with his daggers.

Six steps down, Lena could see the brute gritting his broken teeth at them, his face twisted and scared. It appeared his foot had been healed as he had no problem vaulting up the stairs towards her. She felt a pang of panic rise, but pushed it back down quickly. The brute ignored the other two and came straight for her. It was her job now to finish him so they could reach Karkathi.

The brute bellowed at them in his terrible, deep voice. "My body falls apart!" he screamed at them. "I fly!"

His broad blade slashed through the air, clashing with Lena's two blades as she parried the strike. His eyes were wide and bloodshot, sunken into his red, scarred face. Spittle flew from his mouth, and he pushed his blade harder against hers, screaming in her face.

"The sky falls. The beast herds stampede. Leaves fall into molten rivers!"

Now Lena realized that the man was not only big and strong but also insane. Judging by his bloodshot eyes and the potent smell coming from his mouth, coupled with the fact that his wound wasn't bothering him, Lena guessed he was on some sort of hallucinogen for the pain.

She pushed him back with all her strength, and he stumbled down a few tiers. She could see the other cult members had engaged with Reeve and Dareth. The dwarf had already dispatched one and taken his sword, ditching one of his daggers for the longer weapon that worked as a longsword for his short arms.

She didn't have time to see how Reeve was faring as the brute regained his footing and charged back up at her. She was happy she had the high ground, as it put her on a more equal footing with the man who towered over her in their last duel.

Catching his next swing with one sword, she felt the impact reverberate all the way up her arm. She had to ignore the sting as this left him open below for her other sword to land a blow. Bringing her right arm in fast, she aimed the sword at his leg, but he quickly caught on and dropped all of his weight onto his sword, pushing her blocking sword down and catching the attacking sword on the way.

Both of her swords crashed down hard into the ground, and as he picked his sword up to attack again, she realized one of her swords had become stuck in a crack between the stairs.

With no time to wedge it free, she shifted both hands to the free sword and blocked another blow. The brute laughed his guttural, booming laugh as his force knocked her over backwards into a sitting position on the step behind her.

"Molten rivers flow!" he yelled as he brought the sword down in a bashing onslaught. The constant clashing and the laughter drew the attention of Reeve and Dareth.

"Lena!" yelled Reeve, adding more ferocity to his attacks to break himself free of the men he was fighting and reach her before she was cleaved in two by the brute's gigantic sword.

With a loud grunt, the brute brought his attack down on her sword with such strength that her hand popped open from the shock of the reverberation, and she watched helplessly as it clattered down the stairs.

"No!" yelled Reeve, almost free from his attackers.

Lena watched in horror as the brute pulled his sword high overhead with both hands, bringing it swooshing down through the air. She winced and closed her eyes, bracing for the impact, but it never came. Instead, she heard a small exhale in front of her and the sound of metal cutting through bone and flesh. Drops of liquid rained down on her. They were thick, and though she didn't want to admit it, she knew it was a spray of blood.

Opening her eyes, she saw the horror before her as the tip of the broadsword was inches from her face, the rest sticking out of the back of Dareth who had jumped in front of the attack, dagger raised. Terror and awe gripped her as she realized the broadsword hadn't impaled him, but had broken through his blade and entered him from the top of the skull.

The brute pulled his sword free, and what was left of Dareth fell forward and rolled down the stairs down into the bowl of the sanctum.

Before she even had time to realize what she was doing, Lena lunged head and hands first to reach her sword that was still stuck in the steps. She could feel tears running down her face as she screamed to let out the agony, using her fiery emotions to rip her sword free from the stone and up into the stomach of the brute.

He looked down in shock, but then lifted his head to spit blood in her face, smiling with red and yellow teeth. This sent her over the edge, and she screamed again with the effort of yanking the sword out and bringing it around in one powerful movement.

Her sword cleaved the brute's head right from his body, and she watched as his still-smiling face rolled down the stairs. His body crumpled with an enormous thud. Lena let out a cry over what had just happened, unable to get all of her emotion out.

With the brute's massive form gone now, she could see Karkathi down below, his staff sticking out of the remaining captive scout dwarf, his job of sacrifice complete. Though he didn't look at all happy about it. He was staring at the head of his brute as it came to a stop by his feet. Then he looked up, mouth agape, at Lena. She stared daggers back at him, anger and fury in her eyes, and a snarl on her lips to let him know he was next.

She took two steps down when she heard a cry from her right. Reeve was in trouble as those Dareth had been fighting now set in to attack him.

Not about to lose another companion, she turned on heel and scooped up the sword Dareth had been fighting with, charging straight into the crowd of cult members. She sliced down two of them and met Reeve in the center, standing back-to-back with him as they ran through their aggressors.

When several more had fallen, the others looked down to Karkathi for support, but he was no longer there. Seeing they were outmatched and their leader had fled, the remaining four cultists ran down the stairs and out through a doorway on the other side of the room.

Looking down at the scene below them, Lena could see the stairs littered with bodies, the most noticeable being the headless brute at the bottom. Walking slowly down the stairs, she found where Dareth lay, crumpled unceremoniously in a heap.

She had never been a big fan of dwarves, yet here lay one who had saved her life twice. The second time having given his own life to save her. Her hand shook uncontrollably. She felt Reeve place his hand on her shoulder. Frantic rambling spewed forth from her mouth so much that even she didn't know what she was saying.

Tears welled in her eyes, and her legs would no longer support her.

In the dimly lit chamber surrounded by death, Lena dropped to her knees, tears bursting forth, and she violently broke down.

CHAPTER SIXTEEN

REASONS TO FIGHT

She wasn't aware of how long she had stayed there sobbing. All she knew was that Reeve didn't leave her side the entire time, his arm gently placed around her shoulders to console her. Not that anything could console her at this moment.

Lena kept thinking about all the prejudice that had been instilled in her life about dwarves by her father. He was always willing to help humans, but with dwarves, he'd always told her she should avoid them. Don't help them, because they'd never help you.

But had he ever really had any experience with them? She didn't know, but it was nothing like she'd just experienced, she was sure. In fact, she doubted his experiences were ever anything like what she'd been through. Being a powerful magical user, it was likely he simply blew Vairtross into oblivion with no actual fight or even a concern if there were innocents inside. Yet here he had sent his magically inept daughter right into a war zone without a care.

And Dareth? Poor Dareth. All he'd wanted to do was save the dwarves from the mines, and not only had they failed to save a single one, but he had willingly sacrificed himself for her, an elf he'd just met.

It was several minutes before she even realized that she was rambling and saying most of this out loud between sobs. She assumed it was mostly incoherent to Reeve, but he patted her on the back and said, "It's okay, Lena. Dareth was a good companion. He did what he had to do. He did what I would have done if I could have gotten to you in time."

Lena wiped her eyes and looked up at him, into his deep blue eyes. There was such kindness there. Such caring. Things she hadn't seen in any of the elves back home, not even in the females. Everyone there was so focused on training for the exact thing she was going through now, and suddenly she realized that the training could never prepare any of them for what it was actually like battling against dark magic. Watching sacrifice and pain unfold before your eyes.

"We have to make sure they can't hurt anyone else," said Lena, regaining her composure. "I want them dead for what they did to Dareth and the Tahlari, but it's more than that.

They will keep killing and sacrificing until they get what they want. And right now, they want your whole family dead."

Reeve nodded at her solemnly. "Yeah," he said, distantly. "Both sides of my family, it seems."

This sentence hung in the air for a moment before Lena could gather herself enough to connect the dots. "So you are Tahlari? It's not just an honorary title?"

Reeve nodded. "We should get out of here and let the dead rest," he said. "I will tell you more along the way."

"We can't just leave them!" Lena pleaded, daring a glance at Dareth.

"We must," said Reeve. "We don't have time for a proper burial. We have to find Karkathi and his sorcerer and put a stop to this."

Lena knew he was speaking sense, but still couldn't bear it. She spoke a silent prayer to Solana to protect and guide the spirits of the fallen, straightened out Dareth's body next to the line of other dwarves, and then followed Reeve out the back of the room and up a long stone staircase.

Unlike the stairs they had come in on, these stairs looked to be ancient, hewn from the stone that made up the surrounding ground. Lena ventured a guess that this was the official entrance to the sanctum and connected dungeons, likely found later after the cult had found the back way next to their camp and built a makeshift wooden staircase to access the dungeons of Vairtross.

As they climbed the stairs, Reeve told her his story, keeping an arm around her to comfort her as she was still shaking a bit from their ordeal.

"Rasgar is the true heir to the Krollian throne," he began. "Not only is he older, but he's full-blood royalty. Most of the others wouldn't hear of me being chosen as the heir or even being given the title of prince. If my father had skipped Rasgar and chosen me, there would have been a riot. Some think that maybe he still should," Reeve admitted. "Rasgar has a flaring temper and doesn't speak well in front of others. Still, I would never challenge him for the throne. It's not my place."

Lena quietly assured him she was fine and shrugged his arm off her shoulder. He nodded slightly and continued talking. "His mother died when he was very young. My father became depressed. He almost lost his mind. Distraught, he left the mountain and took solace in the woods. He needed to be alone. Needed to gather his thoughts and figure out how he was going to rule someday without a queen."

"That's when my mother found him. She was Tahlari. She took him in and comforted him. Listened to his pain, and helped him talk through his struggles. Because of her, he decided he must go back and face his duty as heir to the throne.

But during their time together, he fell in love, and wanted to take her with him."

Reeve let out an enormous sigh. "My mother was resistant. Not to him, but to the life of royalty. She knew that was his place, but not hers. And she was right. My grandfather was furious that he had taken up with a Tahlari woman. While he saved them in Darmark, he wouldn't hear of them becoming part of the family bloodline. My mother was rejected, and my father went to her."

"That same night he snuck out of the stronghold and back to her once more. He wanted to leave with her, to run away. She rejected him again, knowing his place was up in the mountains. Seems emotions got the better of them, and I was a parting present my mother got nine months later."

They were almost at the top of the stairs now. Lena stopped and looked over at him. "And what happened to your mother? Is she still..." she trailed off.

"Living with the Tahlari? No, she died of an illness when I was very young. I barely remember her. My father had to beg and plead with my grandfather to allow me to live in Mt. Fluore with the rest. I was never allowed to have a title, but I didn't really care. The Krollians are my family, but I'll always have a special connection with the Tahlari. My mother named me Kael 'ed Evania hoping I would be the bridge between the Tahlari tribes and the Kroll family ruling the mountains."

Lena remained silent, taking in what he had said. It framed everything in a new light. No wonder Reeve had been so eager to help. Not only was he protecting his older brother, and heir to the throne, from coming out here into the danger, but he was trying to stop the kidnapping and control of his people. He truly was the bridge his mother had hoped for.

She awkwardly rubbed her injured arm where his strip of tunic was tied, not sure what to say, until something came out she wasn't expecting. "I have a confession as well," she said. Apparently, her subconscious thought it was time to relate.

He looked at her expectantly. "You don't have to tell me anything," he said, holding up his hand to stop her.

"Well, I feel like I do. There's a reason I've been failing every step of this mission..."

"Really...don't..."

"My magic is broken!" she finished, letting the sentence gush out.

To her surprise, Reeve chuckled. If his smile didn't make his face more attractive, she was sure she would have hit him.

"Don't talk nonsense," he said. "Sure, you use your bow and swords a lot, but you've also done some amazing things with magic. Enough to rival the great Umbra!" he said, clapping his hands together.

Now she was sure she was going to hit him. "Those were flukes," she said desperately, wanting him to understand she may not be as much help in the upcoming fight as he'd hoped.

"Oh, come on!" he snapped back. "You neutralized the dogs, you healed Dareth's arm to give him a fighting chance down there. How can you say your magic is broken?"

Reeve pushed the wooden double doors open in front of them, and the cool night air rushed in. They stepped out into the deserted forest, greeted with a wide clearing. Around them lay a broken-down foundation of stone marked out in various squares and rectangles. Piles of stone littered the ground around the foundation. Lena quickly realized it was the remnants of where Vairtross used to stand before her father had blasted it to rubble.

She could feel the cool night air hit her face and ears, telling her she was likely red and flushed from her embarrassment. She hadn't ever told anyone outside of her family about the incident with her sister. Since she may not live through the night, she supposed now was the time.

Crossing her arms in front of her, she looked at the ground as she spoke. "When my sister and I were kids, around twenty and twenty-five..." realizing that would sound odd to a human, she glanced up at Reeve. His eyebrow was raised at her, confused. "That's a young age for elves," she said. "Would probably be equal to eight to ten years old for humans." He nodded, and she looked back down at the ground.

"Anyway, Sable decided it would be a fun idea to try to go swimming in the Dualian Ocean by our kingdom of Zelira. She's overly ambitious and thinks she can do anything. It didn't take much for her to coax me into going to the beach with her that day. She thought it would be fun sister bonding, but I just wanted to go home. I had no idea she wanted to go swimming in the ocean when she invited me."

"It wasn't even the currents or the maelstroms that pulled her under. It was a hydralisk, long thought extinct. One minute she's swimming in the low waves calling for me to join her, the next I see a tail wrap around her and she's gone."

"That must have been terrifying," said Reeve as they walked through the rubble of the remains of Vairtross.

"I didn't have time to register the danger. My only thought was to save my sister. I sprinted into the ocean without a thought or care for my safety. I dove deep, and swam furiously to get her, but the snake had dragged her down too deep. I didn't know what else to do, so I threw my hands out in desperation, grasping for her. That's when light shot from my hands, the first sign ever that I was touched by Solana's magic."

"And you saved her," said Reeve, smiling at her.

"Yes. My magic shocked the snake and let her go. The only problem was that as it shot through the water to escape, its tail smashed me hard in the head, knocking me unconscious. The next thing I knew, I was on the beach with Sable screaming at me, and my father was there. He had an urgent vision that had told him to go to the beach, and that we were in trouble. He revived me."

"Something about the head injury, or the water I had swallowed... something damaged my connection with Solana that day. My magic has been weak since."

"But, clearly you can..."

"I don't know! Okay?" she said more angrily than she'd intended. "It was something about that shrine of Solana. The sacred fountain that multiplies water. It's some sort of beacon, an amplifier. My magic has never felt so connected and whole in my life. Something about The Light in that spot is strong. That's likely why my father built the fountain there. He could sense the connection."

Reeve nodded and tried to put a hand on her shoulder again, but she pulled away. "That's why I'm not sure if I can take on Karkathi and his sorcerer. My bow just doesn't feel like enough."

They made it out of the rubble that was Vairtross and back into the woods, the only place that Lena ever felt at home. "You're the best shot with a bow and arrow I've ever seen," he told her.

She shrugged at him, scrunching her lips to the side, unsure of her abilities. "At this point, I think we should go meet up with the Krollian soldiers at the Virmorph pool. That's likely Karkathi's next move since it's the source of his power to turn Tahlari to his will. Plus, who knows what other powers? We can report back and help them guard it. Hopefully, we'll catch Karkathi as he tries to access the waters."

"Sounds like a plan," said Reeve.

Lena ran her hand along the bowstring across her chest, finding it comforting as always, only this time, the smooth silk made it feel even better. "Let's not let Dareth die in vain," she said, determinedly stomping off through the woods ahead of Reeve, who smiled after her.

CHAPTER SEVENTEEN

DARK REUNION

Fifty soldiers were stationed outside the cave entrance that led to the Virmorph pool. Karkathi watched them as some slept propped against the mountainside, and the others held rank on lookout. Among those who were awake, Karkathi recognized Falton Kroll, brother of King Elric.

The cult leader spat on the ground at the sight. He'd just been alerted that all of his prisoners in the dungeon had been freed by a rogue Tahlari man along with the help of the meddling elf and Reeve. Reeve had been a thorn in his side ever since he'd heard of his birth almost three decades prior. The Tahlari that was born of the royal Kroll blood, and taken from the squalor to go live high in the mountain no less. Karkathi would be happy to see him dead soon.

He stomped on the ground in frustration. The elf and Reeve had ruined so much, and now the source of power he needed to create more Dark Humans was under siege by the very people he was hoping to obliterate. Not to mention that he had hoped that the dwarves he'd sacrificed could make the fabled shadow creatures of Baladan, the Shadruul. These fearsome beasts were beasts of the earth and were much more resilient than dogs or Dark Humans. They were the epitome of Baladan's power.

So far, the creation of these beasts had eluded him. He'd tried humans, both alive and dead. He'd also tried a live dwarf before. This time he had planned to try a dead dwarf, but his plan had been foiled, and all he'd been left with was a sanctum full of dead cult members and dwarves. Not to mention that he was now short Bok. He would have come in handy clearing out this Kroll scum from the Virmorph pool.

His numbers were dwindling, and it had all happened so fast. He now had enough people left back at camp to perform another raid of the Tahlari and get their numbers back up, but if he risked an attack on this squad of well-armed soldiers, even if he won, he would lose.

Not that he wasn't used to losing. He'd lost everything when the Kroll had killed his family, and he was forced to live with the fools that were the Tahlari. Even with the decades he'd spent with them worshipping their god, Solana, Baladan called to him. The dark god always called to him.

He heard him in his sleep. Heard him while he was awake. When he was listening to lectures from his makeshift father, Dallin ed' Suna. Baladan was always talking to him. Whispering about a greater future. A future where he ruled again. A time when peace would reign because of his strict dominance. Not like the weak rule of Solana, where kingdoms were allowed to constantly be at war.

War. It was rumored that Zaroft was heading towards a civil war. The rumors had run rampant, and that's when Baladan had finally told him to set out and find Malak and the other remnants of Vairtross. They had been hiding in the sewers of some southern kingdom like rats, and Karkathi had come with a vision to lead them and free them from their life underground. He was their sign of Baladan's return.

Karkathi had promised them a return to the powerful Virmorph pool, and the eventual rise of Shadruul, and subsequently Baladan himself. He was promised by Baladan that his fate was to end the Kroll, and he knew that meant he would be given rule over Mt. Fluore. To become ruler of all of Zaroft, and eventually Darmark to the south.

And it had all come crumbling down in a matter of hours. All because of...

"That elf," he said aloud, gritting his teeth and punching the nearest tree. The trunk was solid, and the bark scratched his knuckles, but the pain felt good. It was familiar, and he could relate.

He jumped slightly as a voice sounded behind him. "The she-elf is very troublesome indeed." Malak appeared out of the shadows behind him, clutching his staff. "We did not predict she would come. I definitely did not believe she would be such a thorn in our side. Yet here we are, down to less than fifty men, with no way to get to our source of power. What is our next move, Karkathi?" Malak sounded expectant, almost betrayed at Karkathi's failures so far.

"I'm trying to decide how we can take them out without losing any men," said Karkathi, stroking his chin.

Malak sighed. "You promised Baladan was speaking through you, and that Vairtross would be put in its proper place, and at the right hand of you as ruler of the land."

"Yes, I know," Karkathi snapped, pushing his hand out sideways as if to dismiss Malak's negativity. He ran a finger along the waterskin attached to his belt. Suddenly, he felt parched. He dismissed the urge to drink and turned his thoughts back to the only water he truly needed. The water inside the cave. "We just need an edge. We need..."

He trailed off, examining the men guarding the cave a bit closer. Again, one man stood out among the rest. "Oh..." he said, a smile curling on his lips.

Falton Kroll stood with his men by the opening to the Virmorph pool. The darkness pressed in on them, creepy and foreboding.

Forget the fact that his sons had just been murdered in the cave he was guarding, but he did not know what these magic men were capable of. He knew for sure that his men were not prepared for any magic that would be used if the cult attacked and took back the pool they were guarding. They just needed to keep showing a strong front to dissuade an attack altogether.

He'd had a bad feeling in his gut all night. The elf and his nephew Reeve hadn't been heard from since they'd left earlier that day, and Falton was beginning to worry that they'd met a sticky end against these madmen.

His brother Elric would unfortunately know what it was like to lose a son, just as he had a few days prior. It was the worst feeling in the world knowing nothing could bring them back to him, and that the cult who had killed him were still out there.

Silently, he wondered if he and his men should abandon their guard duty and sneak off into the woods. Kill the bastards while they slept and avenge his family. It may not be a bad idea. Take the fight to them before they could come in swinging with magic. Half the guard was now well rested, and a surprise seemed to be the smart move.

Turning to his second-in-command, he motioned for him to come over, but before he could speak, there was a rustling in the woods.

"Fantastic," he whispered, gripping his spear tight and readying himself for a fight. Instead of a group of men, though, he saw three solitary figures approaching.

Falton squinted through the darkness. Was it Reeve and the elf with the dwarf they were meant to find? No, that made little sense. They were all too tall for any of them to be dwarves.

There was a groaning that slowly permeated the air, and it sent a chill down Falton's spine. He squinted hard in the dark until finally the figures got close enough to make out the details of their faces. A wide smile broke out across his face.

"Impossible!" he said with a laugh as he clapped his soldier on the back. "It's Rangston! And he's got Baron and Bucklow with him! Reeve must have been mistaken! He..." Seeing his son walking back to him brought happy tears to his eyes. His smile was so big it felt like it would break his face. But then he realized something was off.

The three figures were now only ten yards away, and Falton's mouth fell open wide. The three young Kroll men were there, but they were hobbling. He saw his son's face, but it really wasn't his son at all. Bloody death wounds still littered the men's bodies, mouths open, gasping in horrified moans as they walked towards Falton and the others.

A shocked moan escaped Falton's lips, and he was frozen in fear. The men around him, those who were awake, saw the horrible sight and froze too, unsure how to react to seeing their general's undead son and nephews walking towards them slowly through the shrouded woods. Their instincts said attack, but they were waiting for orders. Orders that never came.

More figures appeared behind the three men, first as shadows, but then rushing quickly to catch the undead Krollians. With bows raised and arrows ready, the cult members shot down the shocked Kroll soldiers. The last thing Falton saw before the arrow pierced his neck was the look of terror on his undead son's face as he raced towards him, knife at the ready to finish any whom the arrows didn't take down first.

Chapter Eighteen

High Stakes

Torches flickered through the forest beyond the trees, alarming Lena and Reeve when they first caught sight of them. Worry of attack soon dwindled as they realized it was a long line of freed Tahlari with torches running from the dungeons and back to their clans.

Lena pulled her bow as they drew closer to the Virmorph pool cave. Reeve had gone quiet for the last several minutes, and she could see his knuckles were white as he tightly gripped his sword. They both expected to run into Karkathi somewhere along the way, and their sense of foreboding grew every minute they faced empty woods.

She carefully nocked an arrow into her bow as they saw the shimmer of light appear in the distance. They were drawing close to the mountain and weren't sure what to expect when they reached the mouth of the cave. Not seeing Karkathi in the woods gave her a growing sense of anxiety with every step they took.

The glow grew brighter as they approached, and they began to see the shapes of soldiers standing at attention in a semicircle around the cave. She could hear Reeve blow out a sigh of relief at the familiar sight of Krollian soldiers.

"We still hold the cave, so at least there's some good news," said Reeve.

But a few more steps instantly made Lena's mouth go dry, and she almost dropped her bow in shock. She immediately threw out a hand and placed it on Reeve's chest, stopping him from going further.

"It's not what you think," she said, unsure how to tell him.

"Lena," he said, brushing her hand aside and taking a few more steps, "they're right there. I can see my uncle. Everything is..."

His hand shot immediately to his mouth as his eyes finally let him see what was truly in front of them. Sticking up out of the ground were fifty stakes. Each stake was run through the body of a dead Krollian soldier so that they appeared to be standing upright. Large fires lit behind them showed them as silhouettes in the darkness. This made it hard to see the details of their faces, but Lena's elf eyes allowed her to see that their eyes were all wide in horror, their mouths agape in silent screams.

Next to her, Reeve quickly removed his hand from his mouth and turned away from her to retch behind a nearby pine. Just the sight of the dead men was bad enough, but Lena was sure the vomiting was a reaction to noticing his uncle was at the forefront of his soldiers.

"I'm so sorry!" she said, rushing over to him and placing a hand on his back. "We're too late. I'm so sorry." She really didn't know what else to say. Elves lived for thousands of years and had not known war in her lifetime, so she wasn't really sure how to deal with someone grieving the death of a loved one very well.

Reeve wiped his mouth to clear the vomit from his lips and looked Lena square in the eyes. "This has to end now," he said. "The monsters that did this have to be in there now, doing Solana knows what with that dark magic pool. We have to end this before they gather enough force to get to the rest of my family. End it, no matter what the cost."

Lena nodded, helping him get steady on his feet. Even in the darkness, even with the grieving and the horrors that they'd witnessed tonight, somehow Reeves' presence and fierce determination worked to calm her just enough to press on.

With weapons drawn, they approached the mouth of the cave, quickly rushing past the rows of dead bodies. Even as they made their way through them, Lena caught a tear falling from

Reeve's eyes as he caught a closer look at his uncle. He brushed it away with the back of his wrist, and they threw themselves against each side of the cave opening.

Carefully peering inside, Lena could see that the cult was gathered there. Fresh blood ran across the rock that led up to the pool, and to Lena it didn't seem like it was from the Krollian soldiers. The blood trails led right up to the glowing purple pool where the cult stood in the water, snake masks still on and glowing slightly purple from the magic of the pool, attention drawn to Karkathi and his sorcerer on the far side.

"...shall not be set back any longer!" they heard Karkathi yell, fists pumping the air for effect. "The elf girl and Reeve have ruined much of what we've worked for..." Lena's eyes went wide as she heard herself mentioned. She had apparently made an impact tonight, though it didn't feel like any victories had been won.

"...so now we infuse ourselves with the Virmorph. After we use this dark magic, we will rally with those back at camp. With our new power, we'll lead them to march into the woods and take every last Tahlari man, woman, and child, regardless of age. We will bring all the clans and turn them into Dark Humans."

Lena's finger was itching to pull back her bowstring and lay Karkathi down into the pool right now, but she wasn't sure she could get a clear shot with all the cult members in the way.

She also wasn't sure who to shoot first, as Malak still posed an enormous threat as well.

Karkathi continued his speech. "By this time tomorrow, we will march on the mountain from the inside. We will take the Kroll family down!" The surrounding men gave a happy chant of agreement. "We will spill King Elric's insides on the throne room floor!" The responding chant grew louder in agreement.

On the other side of the cave opening, Lena could see Reeve's mouth curl into a snarl as he took a step forward, but she quickly held up a hand for him to wait. His lip twitched at her in anger, but he didn't move.

"After we take the mountain, Baladan will rise!" Karkathi shouted. "This great land we live in will finally know peace!"

The cult's chant rose to an absolute din. Karkathi turned to his sorcerer and gestured his hand towards the pool. "Malak, these men have exposed their very blood to the power of the Virmoph pool. Cast your spell on these waters and bring forth the true power of Virmorphia, that we may honor Baladan and bring justice to our world!"

The sorcerer raised his staff and drifted it towards the pool. As he chanted, the tip of his staff grew brighter. Lena didn't want to know what type of monstrosities would come out of the pool once this ritual was complete, and knew that the time was now or never.

Rolling her back along the cave wall, she spun quickly into the room. The sudden movement made Malak stop lowering the staff and look up at her. Everyone else followed his gaze until the entire group was turned and staring at Lena, bow drawn as she found a clear shot to the sorcerer's neck.

Glancing sideways, she could see that Reeve had come up beside her, sword drawn should anyone dare to come at them.

Karkathi rolled his eyes. "Of course you are here. You're like a gnat that I can't quite squash. You keep buzzing around where you don't belong."

Lena wasn't sure what she was waiting for, but her fingers wouldn't let go of the silk string. She knew there was no reasoning with this madman. She also knew that as soon as that arrow was set free, all hell would break loose, and she needed a minute to figure out what her next move would be.

"You've hurt so many people," she said, stalling. "To what end?"

Karkathi just smiled and laughed. "My entire life was taken from me when I was just a boy. I'm simply righting some wrongs and not allowing Zaroft to fall into the chaos of a civil war. You must understand that our country needs firm leadership, and not the floundering of the weak Krolls."

If she dropped Malak, she could stop the ritual, but if she could get a good shot at Karkathi, the others could lose their will to fight. She thought back to her visit to the Tahlari village and her talk with the chief. Karkathi was an outsider here. Likely Malak's means to an end. Maybe his death was only important to her and Reeve? She still wasn't sure what to do.

"You have no idea what it takes to rule!" Reeve shouted at him.

The madman's smile grew wider. "Ahh. Reeve. The Bridge of the People. Taken from the village to live the life of luxury up above. Keep talking, boy. You will end up like your uncle and grandfather soon enough." Murder flashed in Reeve's eyes, and he raised his sword ever so slightly.

"Don't do it," Lena whispered to him out of the corner of her mouth as she saw he was itching to take the bait and charge forward.

Reeve's lip twitched. Karkathi gestured behind him to the rocks that Reeve had hidden behind when he'd first discovered the cult doing their ritual. "Or maybe you'll end up like your cousins, hmm?"

Lena watched as Malak pointed his staff at the rocks. Groans could be heard filling the cave, and three men stood up. Lena didn't recognize them, but still gasped in horror as their death wounds were clearly visible. The undead men pulled themselves to their feet and walked into the pool to flank Karkathi.

"A bit of a joyous family reunion, wouldn't you say?"

Reeve took the bait this time and lunged forward. Without thinking, Lena stuck her foot out and tripped him, sending him down hard onto the stone floor of the cave. His sword fell from his grasp and went clattering along the ground, splashing into the pool before them.

Karkathi's laugh filled the air. "Kill them!" he yelled. The undead Krollian trio raced through the pool, joined by the other cult members as they all rushed towards Lena and the downed Reeve.

Lena silently cursed herself for missing her opportunity to take at least Karkathi or Malak down first and glanced around for anything that could save them now.

Her eyes settled on the many stalactites hanging from the cave ceiling, like spears overhead waiting to be dropped. She muttered a quick incantation, and the tip of her arrow glowed with a bright yellow light. She could feel her energy drain instantly, and knew it was not a spell she could sustain, but she wouldn't need to.

She quickly pulled her bow up and aimed at the cave ceiling, high past the tips of the stalactites, to the very ceiling of the cave. The arrow whipped from her bow and through the dim cave, lighting its way up to the solid rock above them in a streak of brilliant yellow light.

"No!" Karkathi screamed. The last Lena saw of him, he was turning to run as her arrow found solid rock and exploded overhead. The din of screams was deafening as rock barreled down from the ceiling, the sharp stalactites finding their marks. Those that weren't impaled were crushed by falling rock.

Lena grabbed Reeve by his shirt and pulled him back through the mouth of the cave as rock piled down, burying the cult members and undead Kroll in the pool, and blocking the cave entrance.

They both stumbled backwards and fell hard to the ground as dust from the cave filled the air. For a moment they forgot about the gruesome visage of the bodies on stakes around them as they gathered themselves.

"Are you okay?" Lena asked, helping Reeve to his feet. She could tell as he stood up that he was trying to look anywhere else other than at his uncle.

"For now," he said, dusting himself off. They stood, and Lena slung her bow, putting herself up under Reeves' arm and helping him walk out past the bodies and back into the woods to get away from the gore. With the cave and the massacre behind them, she propped Reeve up against a tree and took some deep breaths to steady herself.

"You think they're all dead?" Lena asked, panting, glancing back at the blocked entrance. "There are other ways out if they survived, right? Should we go back to the dwarves and..."

Another explosion sounded from the cave. Rock debris went flying quickly through the air, and Lena had to pull Reeve around and slam him against the nearest tree as rock whizzed by.

Once the explosion calmed, they slowly glanced around the trunk. There, standing in the mouth of the cave was a lone figure, staff in one hand, and a waterskin in the other.

With a quick look around, the figure didn't appear to see them, and he went tearing off into the night at full sprint. Lena punched the tree and screamed in frustration and anguish. Karkathi had survived the cave-in.

CHAPTER NINETEEN

THE SHRINE

The crunch of dozens of feet stepping on pine needles filled the air as Karkathi led what was left of his cult through the pine forest towards their final destination.

His mind flashed quickly back to the massacre inside the Virmorph cave. The falling rock had buried the pool and everyone in it. Karkathi had dove behind the small rock wall by the pool just in time to avoid being impaled by a spear-like point from above. Malak had not been so fortunate.

As Karkathi peered back over the rock, he had seen the shaman sprawled out on the ground, blood dripping from his mouth, his body stuck with a sharp rock. He was struggling to speak, but couldn't quite make out words, and the old shaman of Vairtross died right before his eyes.

Karkathi didn't have time to dwell on it, and quickly snatched up the staff. The staff was the only logical way out.

Going back through the mountains meant coming across the dwarves, and he doubted he could get by them alive.

The only other thing he needed was to preserve some of the powerful Virmorph liquid to harness the power they needed to raid the Tahlari one last time. He had filled his waterskin and blasted his way out into the night. A quick look around proved that the troublesome elf and the vile Reeve were gone.

Rounding up the last of his Dark Humans and his five remaining cult members from camp, he was now leading them to the one place that would allow them to multiply the power of the little Virmorph liquid they still had.

Karkathi burst out into the clearing and hopped over the lip of the large basin, stopping himself at the bowl beneath the statue of Solana. Resting the staff against the lip of the bowl, he pulled out his waterskin and dumped the water in.

He scowled at Solana's stone smile and then began the chant that his faux father, Dallin, had taught him many years prior to help multiply the water during a long drought. The water in the bowl grew brighter and brighter purple, and it expanded in the bowl, spilling out onto the ground around his feet.

The water expanded until it reached the edges of the lip, running in ripples along the ground, creating a shallow basin of water surrounding Karkathi and the shrine. The warm, purple water washed over his feet, and he felt the tingle of the power course through him.

He turned and waved to the others to join him in the water. They didn't hesitate to step forward as they were beckoned, not that the Dark Humans among them had a choice. It was much shallower than the pool, but the Virmorph liquid surrounded them once again.

Karkathi took a deep breath. It was time to end this, no matter what the cost.

Lena and Reeve came to a stop from their trailing sprint and watched as the party gathered in the basin around the fountain. The glowing purple water lit the otherwise dark area with an eerie glow. Lena shook her head as she saw the statue of Solana on the shrine. The statue had turned from its stone-gray color to black.

"They've tainted it," she whispered, aghast.

"Desecration of The Light with dark magic," Reeve agreed. "We have to stop them here and now. He's getting desperate."

He didn't have to tell Lena twice. She nocked an arrow in her bow and took aim. This had gone far enough. Whatever differences she had with her father, she still had deep respect for her god. Whatever was happening here wasn't natural and had to be stopped.

She let the arrow fly, but right before it sank into Karkathi's back on the left side, he raised the staff, and the arrow froze mid-air.

Lena's lip twitched as she quickly strung another and didn't hesitate in firing. Her aim was so dead on that the tip of the arrowhead hit the other arrow and split it, before it too froze mid-air.

Karkathi slowly turned around with a dark and ecstatic grin on his face. "I assumed I wouldn't be able to complete my ritual without you showing your faces again," he said, acid dripping from his voice. He let the arrows drop into the water at his feet. "The only thing is, this time you are too late."

He slammed the staff hard into the water beneath him, and ripples of green light broke through the purple water. The water reacted by growing brighter purple, so bright that Lena had to shield her eyes.

Moans and yelps of pain could be heard from the other side of Lena's hand. The moans quickly turned to angry barking. The light faded, and as Lena lowered her hand, her worst fears were confirmed. He had turned the cult into the same grotesque dogs they had run from earlier that night.

Cackles from the dogs filled the air, but the laughing dogs that began to slowly form a circle around them wasn't even the most horrifying part. In the middle of the circle by the fountain stood Karkathi, though he no longer resembled a man. He wasn't quite a dog either.

Instead, he stood a full three feet taller than he had been before. His body was bulging with powerful muscle and dark fur. Out of his back shot the same red semi-luminescent spikes that protruded from the other dogs. He still stood on his hind legs, where the others were on all fours, towering above his subordinates.

His thin snout had the same haunting mouth that hinged in the back just a little too far to be normal, allowing his mouth to hang open with a gaping maw ridden with needle-like teeth.

His eyes glowed red as he stared down at them, his chest heaving as he breathed heavily, relishing his new power and how small his foes now looked below him.

"This form will do for now," he howled, stretching his muscular arm out to the side and examining his new claws, flexing the fingers as if to test out his new body. He took a few steps towards them, and Lena nocked another arrow. Reeve pulled the sword from Lena's right sheath and put himself between her and Karkathi, though she wasn't sure how much good he could actually do against such a beast of a man.

"All will fear me as a beast," he growled. "Nothing will stop my might!"

Lena took quick aim at his eye and fired off her arrow. Karkathi easily side-stepped the projectile as if it were a pesky bug that simply annoyed him more than a weapon that threatened him.

She could sense the smaller dogs pressing in tighter around them as Karkathi slowly made his way closer. She quickly slung her bow and pulled her remaining sword, bracing for impact.

Karkathi raised his claws, but before he could do anything, Reeve charged forward, sword swinging. His blade caught the beast-man's arm, and he roared in pain, though the cut looked to be shallow. It still angered Karkathi, so he swung his right arm across and caught Reeve in the head. Reeve went staggering backwards and down into the Virmorph pool, sword clattering through the shallow water and landing by Lena's feet.

She had just enough time to pick it up when Karkathi snapped his fingers. The dogs all rushed at once, and Lena dipped into her fighting stance, ready to strike the first one that reached her.

As two dogs jumped to take her on, time seemed to freeze. No, not quite frozen. The dogs were still moving, but it was at an insanely slow pace. She marveled at the spectacle of the slow dogs for a moment, before her eye caught a yellow beam of light. It was coming from the statue of Solana. It was shining towards her, and then seemed to bounce off, tracing arcs through the air towards the closing dogs.

In an instant, she understood what it meant. It was her path of attack. Bringing her swords through the air and following the beams of light in the eerie purple darkness, she sliced through the first two dogs, and they slowly fell to the ground.

The light played across the air, lining up her strike for the next one that was heading her way. After this, she saw the three that were surrounding the unarmed Reeve, who was still on the ground, and the light path showed her exactly how to take them out before they could pin him down and rip his throat out.

Reeve didn't seem to know what was going on, as he too was moving in slow motion. Blood moved through the air in slow-motion streaks and droplets from the fresh cuts on the dogs. They moved impossibly slow, and Lena had a second to marvel at the drops almost hanging in midair before the light arced again, this time towards Karkathi's throat.

She happily raised her sword, glad that Solana was showing her the way to end all this madness. She gave a battle cry as she swung the sword with all her might at the beast's exposed throat.

Just as she thought she had her mark, the sword smashed into something solid, and she felt a familiar reverberation spread up her arm.

"Enough!" Karkathi screamed, his staff raised to block her deathblow. They stood locked for a moment before the beast pushed back, forcing her back a step. She quickly regrouped and squared off against him again.

"I am the messenger of Baladan, Elf. Do not think that your tricks will work on me."

She gritted her teeth. Her mind flashed back to the symbol she had seen in the dungeon. The symbol of the snake and the quill. Baladan's symbol, and the whisper. 'You will fail,' the voice had told her. It rang loudly in her ears as if she were hearing it again.

All of her fears came flooding back. She suddenly felt out of her league in this fight. She was fighting a hellhound beast of Baladan, which was counteracting Solana, and she couldn't even use proper magic. What good were swords against such evil?

Karkathi brought the staff down swiftly toward her head, and she pulled both swords up in an 'X' to block. She quickly brought the blades across, hoping to sever the staff in half, but they simply slid off, not even leaving a mark.

The beast drew the staff into the air, a green light igniting from the top. He brought it down to point at Lena, and she barely rolled out of the way as the green light shot past her.

She charged low, hoping to strike his legs and stifle his quick mobility, but he brought the staff down hard on her swords, driving them down to ricochet off the water basin below them.

Lena brought one sword up fast and dug the tip into Karkathi's free arm. He pulled the staff across and knocked the sword loose, but bellowed in pain as red blood spilled through the air.

The injury angered him, and he bludgeoned her with a mix of hard hits and magical blasts that she narrowly dodged while parrying the blows that came her way.

She worked her way in close enough that he could not point the staff to blast her, and made him play her game, which was good old-fashioned fencing. Though he was strong, her rage and determination were enough to hold his attacks back.

At one point she glanced to the side and saw that Reeve was back on his feet, though he was grappling bare-handed with an attack dog. Panic gripped her as another dog came in to knock him over, while the first went for his throat.

Looking even for this moment was enough to distract her from her fight, and Karkathi brought his staff up hard into her chin. Her eyes exploded into a blur of stars as they watered over from the impact.

Seizing his chance, the beast brought the staff across, knocking her swords from her hand, and with another thrust into her chest, he knocked her over backwards.

Lena fell hard with a splash into the Virmorph basin, her hand catching her fall on the hard rock. Pain shot through her right wrist. It wasn't broken, but the impact had sprained it. The water felt warm, and she could feel the liquid as it permeated the burn she had gotten on the back of her hand in Petaro. It felt like the dark magic was working its way into her, and she knew she had to get up fast.

Ignoring the pain, she unslung her bow and stood in one motion, and in another she reached for and nocked an arrow and spun to face the beast that was Karkathi ed' Sayana.

Only she couldn't let her arrow fly, for Karkathi was no longer alone. Having seen her draw her bow, he had quickly snatched Reeve from the other dogs. He was now crouched down and holding Reeve tightly against himself, using him as a meat shield.

Her eyes grew wide with fury as she stared down the beast that was peering from just out behind Reeve. Reeve himself didn't look afraid, but more worried that Lena wouldn't take the shot because of him.

"Give up, she-elf!" Karkathi screamed from behind Reeve. "I know what damage you can do with that bow, and you wouldn't want this halfling to die, now would you?"

Lena's fingers twitched on the bowstring. The best she could do from this angle was shoot him in the shoulder as he was much broader than Reeve. The shot definitely wouldn't take him out.

"What do you want?" she spat at him angrily. She could see Reeve slowly shaking his head, signaling her not to bargain.

"I want you to take your human lover here, and leave these woods. Go back home. Never return. This mountain, and soon this entire land, belongs to me," he snarled.

"Just shoot him, Lena!" Reeve yelled at her. "Drop us both!"

She could hear the snarling of the smaller dogs as they slowly shrunk their circle around them. They were cult and Tahlari Dark Humans alike, all turned and set to attack her if she hesitated much longer. Even if Karkathi killed Reeve and she got a good shot in, these dogs would still kill her on the spot. She couldn't let the cult survive this.

She spoke in tongues. It began as a whisper, but quickly grew louder. Karkathi's eyes widened as he saw her bow light up with magic. The tip of the arrow glowed bright yellow, and to her surprise, glowing runes were now etched along the limbs of the bow, adding yellow light to the scene to counteract the purple glow and add power to her shot.

Past Karakthi she could see the statue of Solana radiate yellow as well. For whatever reason, her connection with this statue amplified her powers. For the first time in her life, Lena truly felt like Solana was with her.

"I'll blow us all up if you don't let him go!" she yelled as the spell finished. The dogs stopped moving in, afraid of the glow that radiated from her weapon. Karkathi's eyes were darting around, weighing his options. Even if his dogs killed Lena now, the bow would drop and likely explode, regardless.

"Do it!" yelled Reeve as Karkathi walked backwards. He was slowly inching his way towards the statue, aiming to jump behind it and run.

Reeve locked eyes with her, the desperation set in his gaze. She stared hard into his deep blue eyes, seeing the future they had together that never could be, and that never could have been since the beginning.

"This is your fate, Lena!" he called to her, struggling hard against Karkathi's hold. "Take the shot!"

They were now by the statue of Solana, and Karkathi reached up with his massive paws towards Reeve's chin and the top of his head. Reeve contorted his face at the assault. Panicked, Lena let loose her arrow. The golden light streamed across the dim purple darkness and right towards her target.

Her life flashed before her eyes as she knew the explosion would kill them all. As the yellow light cut through the purple glow of the basin, she saw her mother that she would never get to say goodbye to. Her brothers, who would miss her camaraderie. Her father's disappointment at her failure tonight. And her sister. Her sister, who had a full life because she had sacrificed so much of her own life to save her.

This last thought brought a smile to Lena's face, and she watched as the arrow sank into Karkathi's shoulder. She dropped her bow, and it fell, as if in slow motion, as the arrow exploded in a ball of light and began its outward motion to consume everything around it. Lena caught one last look at Reeve. She could see pain etched on his face as he squinted against the light and the brief flicker of pain from the explosion. She saw in his eyes the pain of not living to see whether the country would be united, or would fall during a civil war. To see if his family would be okay without him.

Then, he dissolved into the light.

The sphere of energy was vaporizing everything in its path, and though it seemed slow to her, she knew she couldn't run away from the incoming danger. She knew she didn't want to. Her bow hit the ground with a splash by her feet, and she dropped her arms to her side, palms out, ready to embrace her end as Reeve had.

Dogs vaporized in front of her. She closed her eyes, bracing for the impact. It was then that she felt a tingle run up her arms. She had expected it to burn more, but then she realized it wasn't the explosion that was taking her.

Both arms shot up in the air against her will. Confused, she tried to put them back down, but they hung in the air as her own sphere of light erupted from her hands. Somehow, through the explosion, she could see the statue of Solana twinkle to life, feeding her power and her automatic reaction to shield herself from danger.

"No!" she yelled as the shield sprung up around her. The explosion pushed against her shield, and she watched in anguish as she was saved, and everything else around vaporized before her eyes.

Her eyes were wide with horror. She didn't deserve to live. Not after the sacrifice Dareth had made for her. Not without Reeve. She deserved to die with them. To end all of this cleanly. She had to die with them.

Time sped up, and the explosion ran its course. Lena found herself standing alone in the middle of the shallow water basin. The water no longer glowed purple, the only light coming from her accidental shield. Even the statue of Solana was gone. Suddenly, her shield died out, leaving her staring out into the pitch-black woods. All she could do was scream into the void, but no one else but her was left to hear it.

As her scream of anguish eventually died, there was only silence. Somehow, that was even worse than the scream.

Chapter Twenty

BURY AND BUILD

S he didn't know how long she stood there in the darkness. Time had ceased to exist.

Was this the same darkness Reeve was experiencing right now? Was he with Solana?

She wasn't even sure where she should go. Should she go tell the Kroll family what had happened? Maybe it was appropriate to give Dareth a proper burial? Perhaps it just made the most sense to leave and tell her father what had happened. He could send an official report back to Mt. Fluore so they knew what happened. She wasn't sure she could face them after what had happened anyway.

"Bury and build," said a voice in the darkness.

Lena's eyes were adjusting to the darkness by now, but she saw no movement in the clearing. Given the words, she knew no one was there, but that she was being spoken to from beyond once again.

"What does that mean?" she asked the darkness desperately.

A faint light began glowing in the distance. She could see it was at the center of where the shrine had just stood before she had obliterated it with her magic arrow.

The voice remained calm as it explained. She could tell now that the voice was coming from the light. "Bury what is left of this cult of Baladan. Build a temple to me where light now shines."

Bury the cult? She glanced around in the dim light and saw a few remnants of the dogs that had now transformed back into men since they had died; both cult and Tahlari alike.

And to build a temple? She couldn't even piece together a small statue. "I think you have the wrong elf," she said. "My power isn't what you think it is." She realized after she said it, it sounded dumb, because Solana would know everything.

"Your power is exactly what I think it is; it's just not what you think it is," said the voice calmly. "Your power is strong with me here. Build a golden altar here in the middle, topped with a basin for water, as was here before. Surround it with a temple that reaches the heavens, and rooms for people to gather. Make a dungeon for my enemies and those who do wrong to my people. And hanging from the ceiling, make a statue in my image. Large and grand, to protect those in harm's way. Bury and build for me."

Seriously? What was the fascination with building statues?

"I understand," she answered. "But where can I get enough material to build such a large temple?"

The night was silent. She waited, but there was no answer.

"Okay," she said, approaching the small ball of light where the shrine had been. She placed her hands in the light, and she could feel the power of Solana's Light course through her. "Solana, give me the power to do your will," she prayed.

A warm feeling coursed through her, and she knew she could now do what needed to be done. Without a shovel, she began removing the earth where the stone basin and the shrine had sat. She set aside the shattered rock from these that would help to make the temple.

When the hole was big enough, she gathered the cult, as well as the unfortunate Tahlari men, and laid them all to rest.

She thought about those that were buried in the rock by the Virmorph pool in the mountains and realized that they were already buried in their own graves. Poor Dareth and the other scout dwarves, along with the cult and Tahlari down in the dungeons of Vairtross, were another matter she'd have to deal with later.

Then she thought about Reeve and Karkathi. There was nothing remaining of them to bury as they were at the center of the blast. She felt a pang of guilt at still being alive. The last she saw of Reeve, it looked like Karkathi was about to snap his neck, and he likely would have died anyway. She would never know if this were true.

Feeling there was no one left that needed burying from the clearing, she filled in the area with the dirt she had removed, completing the first of Solana's wishes of her. "Let me know if I'm not doing something right," she said to the darkness, but no one answered.

"Right then," she said as she stalked off into the woods in search of stone for the temple.

The only thing that she thought would work would be to strip the remains of the old Vairtross ruin of its stone. The foundation still held plenty of stone where it outlined the kingdom that her father had destroyed. She imagined that over the years most of the other rubble had been stripped by the dwarves and others, but there was plenty there for her to use.

Using her magic, she ripped huge chunks of stone from the ground and easily moved them back to her construction site. The magic in her never seemed to fade, and she began to wonder if Solana had healed her ailments. Even as the temple rose, she felt strong with The Light, and didn't want the feeling to end.

As dawn broke, she found herself back at the entrance to the dungeons where Dareth and the other dwarves' bodies were. A tear fell, and she realized she couldn't bear to relocate their tomb. Instead, she said a silent prayer and covered both entrances to the dungeons with rubble, and then layers of dirt. Grass and plants would eventually grow there and cover up their death with new life.

Night turned to day, and then night again as she worked diligently on the temple. The circular atrium formed around her, and the tower began to rise. Her magic easily carved the stone perfectly smooth, except where she deemed necessary to carve a decorative flourish.

Rooms were added to the upper levels as instructed, and impossibly smooth and intricate stairs led to each new level that wrapped around the main chamber. Even the dungeons were exquisitely polished, with a large landing between floors where a guard could sit on duty, though Lena had no idea who would even use this temple in the middle of the forest.

As she put together the impossibly colossal statue of Solana that she decided would hang from the ceiling and reach down to those worshipping as the shrine had done, she tried to use the stone she'd set aside from the old shrine and basin. It only seemed fitting that this material made up the bulk of what was essentially a new shrine dedicated to the god.

Through her magic, she made his robes a beautiful golden color trimmed in sapphire-blue. On the ceiling, she painted a scene of the heavens to appear as if Solana was coming down from the sky to greet worshippers.

As she finished the temple, she looked around with satisfaction at her work, until she noticed the dim light that was still in the middle of the atrium where the original shrine had been. Solana's presence was still there, and still silent. It took her a moment to realize that she had forgotten something: the golden altar that was promised.

Although the light remained silent and didn't speak further to her, she could feel she knew what Solana's plan was for her to get the gold needed to build the new altar.

"I have to go tell them," she said out loud in the empty temple, lowering her head and trembling.

Lena found herself outside the large oak doors once again. This time, however, there were no loud, booming voices arguing from the other side. Just silence as the guards opened the door for her to enter.

King Elric sat alone at the council table at the opposite side of the room, hands folded in front of his face. Lena noticed his eyes were glistening as if he had been weeping.

"My guards tell me you've come alone, and unfortunately my own eyes confirm this is true," he said. She could see the tears welling in his eyes once again.

All she could do was nod, her chin trembling as she unsuccessfully tried to hold back tears. Her mind wouldn't let her speak as she was so overcome with a flood of sadness at the king's pain.

Seeing she was distraught, Elric rose from his chair and made his way quickly over to her, wrapping his arms around her in a hug. She leaned into him and broke down, feeling tears from the king hit her shoulder.

"He gave everything to save his family... both of his families," she managed to say after a time. "Reeve... Kael... he sacrificed everything."

Elric nodded, understanding that she knew of Reeve's true origins. "His sacrifice will not be in vain, Lena. We will work harder than ever to protect the Tahalri and bring this land together in peace, in Reeve's name."

After more silence, the king spoke again. "You've done well, Lena. It may not seem like it now, but you and your magic have done extraordinary good here. If there is anything I can do to repay you for your bravery and sacrifice, please name it."

Lena wiped away her tears and stepped back to face him. "There's nothing I could ever ask of you after the losses you've suffered, Your Highness."

He nodded in response.

"Solana, on the other hand, has a request you may be of help with," she added.

Lena took one last look around the interior of the temple she had built for Solana. It was grand work, though she still wasn't sure who it was really meant for. She resolved that she might never find out the god's intention behind her building it.

In the center now stood the altar that he had requested. A magnificent gold pillar topped with a basin for holy water. The base had ornate carvings of vines and flowers along the base. The gold from King Elric was gladly given and now served as the central altar of this magnificent temple.

Closing the large wooden doors behind her, she walked off into the woods without looking back at her creation, a specially selected stone tucked under her arm.

She walked in silence until the temple was completely obscured by the trees. With her free hand, she ran her fingers nervously along the silk string of her bow, which was slung across her back. She wasn't good with things like this, but it just felt like the right thing to do.

She quickly dug a little inlet in the dirt to set the large stone. As she called her magic forth, she felt herself growing weaker. Solana had finally decided her work was nearing its end, and was relinquishing her of the extra power he had bestowed upon her.

With the last of her strength, she etched into the stone.

Rest in Peace R.E.
'Bridge of the People'
Noble. Tahlari.
Friend.

She sat down next to the stone on the ground, completely drained, her magical vibrancy dwindled from a roaring flame to a tiny spark. No tears came this time, just the dead silence pressing in around her as she sat next to the memorial of Reeve. Glancing at her arm that had been cut in the mines, she pulled the piece of Reeve's blue tunic free from her wound and clenched it tightly in her hands. She had hardly known him, but somehow she still missed him deeply. She wasn't even sure what the feeling was, only that it was empty.

"Was this what fate had intended?" she asked the surrounding darkness. "Was this all you had planned for me, Solana?" Still, there was no answer. She picked some grass from the ground and tossed it towards the stone, watching it flutter down to the ground, weightless and without purpose, much as she felt now.

EPILOGUE

H ome had never been the same to her after that mission. Her father had welcomed her back with open arms and congratulations on her mission, but he had become a little colder to her after he'd heard word that the Kroll family had lost many family members and soldiers in the struggle.

It wasn't as clean a job as he had done with Vairtross, and she knew that he secretly wondered if the death had damaged their relationship with the Kroll family.

Her classmates, on the other hand, were very impressed that she had taken on such a daring mission. Her father had likely spread word about it to give her better standing at the academy, and she enjoyed a brief reprieve of people not being completely awful towards her as the rumor spread. It was a short-lived win, however, when her weak magic again made her the joke of the school for the rest of her time there. They all assumed the story had been embellished based on her ongoing weak performance.

Moryan, her betrothed, was happy to see her back, but he could see that she was a changed elf. It was he who broke off their engagement, much to her father's chagrin, but Lena was always grateful to Moryan for taking the heat on their breakup, and for never telling her father about her vision.

As for all of Zaroft, civil war eventually broke out, and much blood was lost as the kingdoms fought. It was a long, bloody war that took place over the course of a century, finally ending when the Kroll family stepped in and brokered the peace they had so longed for. So grateful were the kingdoms that they all agreed unanimously to rename the land after the family's newly adopted surname: Evania.

Lena eventually left her home kingdom of Zelira after her mother had her exiled. She wasn't entirely sure, but she felt that her mother was being corrupted by the same darkness that had made her father eventually fall to Baladan's teachings. The vision Solana had given her father years prior had driven him insane, and he slowly abandoned The Light.

Now, almost two-thousand years old, Lena was venturing back out into the world again, this time to stay. She had traveled little in her time, too afraid of what horrors awaited her in the world. Because of this, her soul told her there was only one place she could really go in her exile.

The pine forest brought a rush of memories back to her, and she pulled her lavender hood down off her graying head to enjoy the forest breeze and the smells that were familiar, and yet somehow so distant.

She had no idea what to expect of the forest surrounding the mountains as she had been away for the span of a few dozen human lifetimes. The Evania family had passed through many generations since Reeve, his name now only a memory in a book somewhere still in the mountain. If any of the Evania family knew his name from history, it didn't matter anymore. The entire Evania family had been wiped out by a tyrannical emperor who now ruled inside the mountain. It was partly for this reason that she felt something calling her here.

Cutting through the woods, she could see the outline of her temple through the trees. A small smile crept onto her face as she saw it. Her creation had stood the test of time. To her surprise as she drew nearer, other buildings popped up through the trees, though none nearly as tall as her temple.

Breaking through into what used to be a clearing, Lena saw that a small town now stood there. There was nothing spectacular about the town other than its temple. The houses and businesses were modest in size and design. The existence of the town now made sense of the potato farms she had seen on the way here.

Walking through a few rows of houses, she found that an enormous square was centered in the town, her temple the focal point of it all. The cobblestone square was filled with all types of vendors selling their wares. People bustled about, busy trading their goods.

On the opposite side of the square, she caught sight of a tavern. It looked newly built, and had a sign hung out front that read 'Tobi's Tavern'. Outside the tavern she saw a young dwarf sternly talking to a dark-skinned girl, and the girl ran off to fetch whatever he had asked for.

A half-smile crept to her lips. All of this was here because of her, because of what she had built. It was surreal to see how it had all come together, but apparently this had been Solana's vision all along.

Not even stopping to check out her temple, Lena headed through town to the one place on her mind that she absolutely wanted to visit. The houses thinned out again until just one small cottage rested near the edge of where the woods picked up again.

Outside the cottage, a middle-aged man sat by a fire. On the fire she could see he had all manner of plants spread out on a griddle, being dried out.

When the man caught sight of her approaching, his face lit up. "Welcome, stranger! Not too often do we get to see elves around these parts!" he laughed as he scratched his long nose. His facial features reminded Lena a bit of a goblin.

"It's been a long time since I've traveled around these parts," she said. "It's good to be back. I'm looking for a new place to settle."

The man smiled at her. "Graeton is as good a place as any! Plenty of open houses in town as the Emperor's last raiding party unfortunately created some vacancies." He scoffed at his own mention of the emperor.

"Thank you," she said, "but I prefer to live in the woods."

"Hmm. No houses available there," said the man.

Lena laughed. "I'm good with building," she said, waving to him as she made her way past his house and back into the pine trees on the other side.

The trees grew thicker again, and it wasn't long until she had found the spot where she would build her new home. She recognized it because, beyond all belief and all reason, there in the ground still stood the stone, her memorial to Reeve, the man who truly was the best of the Krollians and the Tahlari. Time had aged the stone, and the words were barely legible, but it was there all the same.

She sat next to the stone as she had done all those years ago, but this time the emptiness was gone. This time, she felt something stir within her, and a smile reached her lips.

"I'm finally home," she said, running her hand along the silk string of her bow that was dutifully strapped to her back. She was home, and in her heart she knew it was true.

ENJOYED TAHLARI? LEAVE A REVIEW!

YOUR FATE DEPENDS ON IT!

Okay, maybe your **actual** fate isn't at stake... but your review **does** help keep the story alive! Reviews tell the mystical forces of the algorithm that *Tahlari* is worthy of being seen by more adventurers.

Whether you **loved it, laughed at it**, or **threw the book across the room in emotional distress**, I'd love to hear your thoughts! Just a few words can help more readers (and maybe future Dungeon Lords) discover the journey.

Review on Amazon
dungeonlords.com/tahlari/

Ready to enter the full saga?

The story isn't over for Lena...

Start the full-length novel *Dungeon Lords: The Lost Disciple* and witness what happens next.

She's faced the darkness and been exiled from her home.

Now, Lena finds herself exactly where she needs to be, the small town of Graeton, when a mysterious lion-man barrels into town, changing her and her companions' lives forever.

Their mission to save the life of a little girl soon becomes a struggle to decide the Fate of Evania itself.

Available Now:
dungeonlords.com/the-lost-disciple/

STAY
UP-TO-DATE
WITH DUNGEON LORDS

Get exclusive behind-the-scenes content, early access to future launches, and special bonuses only for subscribers! As a member, you'll unlock sneak peeks, deleted scenes, exclusive lore, and even chances to win signed books, art, and other epic rewards. Don't miss out on contests, insider news, and surprises from the world of Dungeon Lords.

dungeonlords.com/newsletter/

ABOUT THE AUTHOR

J.B. Coleman is a lifelong gamer and fantasy storyteller, with a love for **RPGs, medieval worlds, and immersive lore**. He's been writing since **Junior High** and has a background in **SEO and digital marketing**. Now, as the author of *Dungeon Lords: Fate of Evania*, he's excited to take the **Dungeon Lords legacy** to the next level. He lives with his **four children**, balancing **family, writing, and gaming** — always ready for the next adventure.